Nic —
This is a
book. I b. . .
it for people like you. 😊

NOWHERE TRAIN

The Enders, Vol. 1

ALLIE BURKE

[signature] Allie Burke
xo xo

Booktrope Editions
Seattle WA 2015

**Inquiries about additional permissions
should be directed to: info@booktrope.com**

Cover Design by Shari Ryan
Edited by Laura Bartha

Print ISBN 978-1-62015-764-0
EPUB ISBN 978-1-62015-785-5

Library of Congress Control Number: 2015903450

For Jay

"But in fact, depression is not a side effect of cancer. Depression is a side effect of dying. Cancer is also a side effect of dying. Almost everything is, really." –John Green

ACKNOWLEDGMENTS

My riches come in friends and loved ones and supporters, and there are so very many of you that I can't even imagine how I got to be so lucky.

I have the most amazing readers in the world. As with every single piece of literature I put out, your book love shocks me. Thank you for staying with me for so long.

So thankful for Katherine Sears and Ken Shear at Booktrope, for continuing to support my art with the most creative flair. Life as an author feels less and less like a job with every project I am lucky enough to publish with this amazing group. I am so honored to be a part of it.

Rachel Thompson, Nicole Lyons, and the endless list of Stigma Fighters who support everything I do, your support inspires me every single day. From the beat of my heart, thank you. And very importantly, Sarah Fader, for convincing the entire world of my sanity on a daily basis, I love you so much. Thank you for being a part of my world.

Nicholas Denmon, Jennifer and Tymothy Longoria, Sean Sweeney, my oldest friends in the business, I love your words and your faces. I feel so blessed to have you in my life then, now, and as long as you'll have me.

Marni Mann, you are my soul sister. I don't even know what else to say. Wine.

My brother Jason, without whom I would have never written this series, thanks for your awesome notes on that first chapter and also for your awesome brotherdom.

My friend Eric, for not only keeping me grounded in the world outside of fiction, but for asking about word count on a daily basis. B, for asking about books even though I know you don't really give a shit, Jennifer who reads slow except if it's my book, and Alfredo who is still convinced that I have a PhD in Being a Human.

The amazing Shari Ryan, for bringing my words to life in these gorgeous images that not even I can imagine, there really are no words to express how I feel about you, our friendship, your gorgeous writing, or your ethereal talent to bring books to life. You are one of the most talented humans I have ever met.

Dane Cobain and Heather Faville, who have been two of the biggest supporters of my artistic choices this year; I cannot thank you enough for believing in me as an author and getting the word out.

My Editor, Laura Bartha, you are the force that makes my brain-thoughts readable. I still owe you a dollar.

To ALL the amazing people who make this life possible, thank you. I will be forever grateful.

witch
wiCH

noun
noun: witch, plural noun: witches
1. A woman thought to have evil magic powers. Mythical.

Enchanter.
en/chahn/ter

noun
noun: enchanter, plural noun: enchanters
1. A male or female member of a society of humans who can control, manipulate, and change the elements. Real.

Ender.
en/der

noun
noun: ender, plural noun: enders
1. Flesh-eating humans; zombies. Definitely real.

Gunner.
gun/nuhr

noun
noun: gunner, plural noun: gunners
1. A member of the society of post-apocalyptic earth who believes as we all believe at our cores: fight or die. Survival of the fittest.

Holie.
hoe/lee

noun
noun: holie, plural noun: holies, abbreviation for: holistic
1. The "other" society whose members choose a natural, holistic path of life, including the decision to communicate not with words, but with energy and healing. Unwillingly at war with the Gunners when attacked.

Fire.
Family Name: Hadley
Color: Crimson
Origin: Evelyn
Present Day: Elias
STATUS: DECEASED

Water.
Family Name: Brooks
Color: Violet
Origin: Lila
Present Day: Elizabeth, Annabelle, Jane, Abby
STATUS: DECEASED

Wind.
Family Name: Clarke
Color: Black
Origin: Salvador
Present Day: Lewis, Irena, Marni, Daniel, ( )
STATUS: HUMAN

Earth.
Family Name: Reed
Color: Emerald
Origin: Adam
Present: Nolan, Christian, Evan, ( )
STATUS: ACTIVE

PROLOGUE

THE WORLD WAS CALM.

She remembered the expression *calm before the storm* in Prius, but she should've been scared. He should've been scared. The world should've been fucking scared, but it wasn't anymore.

If you saw the scene from outside their aura, the woods could've been a beach, and he could've been her boyfriend in some *Lifetime* movie. No Enders, no Gunners; Holies didn't even have to be a thing in this moment.

She looked over at him, and he stopped, as if he were waiting for her eyes. She took in the bun of long brown hair spun perfectly on the top of his head, snaking her fingers around his neck and running her thumbs up his beard. He gently pushed her against a tree and touched her face with the feathers that were his fingertips.

"I need you to save him."

She couldn't find the words. She never had to before he came into her life.

"I haven't done anything like this in a really long time. I need your help. Please."

"Who will save you?"

He smiled. "My love, I am untouchable. Except by you."

CHAPTER 1

THE WORLD WAS DIFFERENT.

Today, that is. Obviously, the world was different. It had been for years. But today, the world was more different than it would ever be again.

The sky was dark despite the morning hour. The line that separated the sky and the murky water was practically undiscernible. The sun was up there, somewhere, but its rays didn't reign like they once did. They no longer held the power to break through the thick layers of death in the sky. They used to, but that was before zombies, called Enders, took all that away.

After The End, every morning the sun would bleed its insides all over the sky, painting the clouds red. Carmen, Jetilyn Fournier's younger sister, used to ask Jett if the world had been turned upside down when she'd look up at the sky. If, for every Ender who died, the sun would bleed from above instead of the soulless carcass bleeding onto the ground below. The world had indeed shifted backwards, but Jett couldn't tell Carmen that. For that was a secret between her and Chris. Once upon a time, the sun's rays glowed when a new life was born, or that's how it felt to Jett.

But it wasn't like that now. When a new life was born now, the sky itself cried, hiding under the darkness of its own despair. Everyone cried.

Jett gazed upon the horizon. This place was home, for now, but the Holies didn't call it that. They didn't call it anything. Once upon a time, it was called Malibu, but a place such as this—or any place—that lacked complacency, didn't deserve a name. It was just a shell where people could put their shit.

Jett cringed when the expression bounced around her head like a rubber ball controlled by its momentum. *Holies.* Holies didn't call themselves Holies, at least not in Prius—what life was before zombies took over. It was Latin for *before*, Prius. (As in, before the zombies rose.) They were all just people then, whether or not humanity recognized, or accepted, diversity. Holies got their names in this post-apocalyptic era, and so did Gunners. Now, Jett couldn't even remember how that happened.

She couldn't believe—even in her own mind—that she used the label *Holies* to refer to her own family, and herself, but might as well. The Gunners practically ruled what was left of this world, and that's what they called Holies. It had to be worse, anyway. Being known as the assholes with guns who did nothing but kill and bring war upon society. Never peace. Always war.

Holies communicate with energy via the power of the pineal gland, more commonly known as the third eye. Holie wasn't a religion, but a lifestyle. It was a spiritual experience. It was existence, manifested by humanity and how it was meant to live, as the ancestors of the human race once had.

All except that little zombie problem, of course.

Holie was short for Holistic. Holistics, or Holies, reverted back to the most simplistic living that had existed way before Prius. The Holies used natural remedies for ailments (in this life, anything more severe than what would be considered an ailment would kill you anyway); ate only what they themselves grew, captured, or hunted—providing it was organic (as organic as you could get after The End); embraced the bare energy of each being, the same energy that provided the ideal that the mind, and body, had the ability to heal itself; and lived off the moral not to kill unless protecting yourself, unless it was imperative to survive. Oh, and they didn't talk.

The Holies didn't speak because speaking was unnecessary. Proven by an attainable physical and emotional energetic connection, communication didn't depend on spoken words. They were useless to Grayson, to Jett, and to everyone in their community, except maybe Carmen (Carmen chose to speak regardless, and so, of course did Boyd, her boyfriend). They could tell, *show*, their feelings, their needs, their desire, their love, to each other through energy. Words only got in the way of life and they were one-hundred percent inconsequential. The Holies chose an alternate way of life, after the original way of life had practically eliminated humanity.

Gunners killed people, basically. Gunners killed everybody. That was what they did; how they lived their lives.

It was Holies versus Gunners. It had been for a long time. And regardless of the Holies' peaceful way of life, when it came down to it, not one of them would hesitate to take a Gunner down if it meant protecting one of their own.

In Prius, before Jett and Carmen's mother died, the family of four lived on a suburban street called Church in a town they used to call Devonbrook. People from surrounding towns used to think the residents of Devonbrook were part of some cult because they never spoke to anyone outside. It wasn't that they didn't speak to outsiders, though; it was that they didn't speak to anyone. They didn't speak at all. Except Carmen who never stopped speaking to anyone, including the rest of the world. She refused to be singled out.

Her family—the original Holies, or what was left of them—definitely didn't come up with that name for themselves; it was so stupid. They would never call themselves that. They would never call themselves anything. Names were just labels, and they didn't need to *be* anything. They were who they were, and that was good enough. It was more than good enough. They were the products of their own happiness. They didn't lie; they didn't have to. It was the best fucking life anyone ever knew.

It was a cult, in some ways, a crimeless one. The community grew its own food; the people didn't use chemicals, doctors; they homeschooled their children. And they didn't speak.

They didn't speak because speaking was overrated, only got you in trouble, and because the ability to speak to one another with the auras and energy humans were born with had been masked by years of exposure to fluoride, calcium, and artificial ingredients in food. Jett was aware that Carmen had tried to explain this to her friends in Hazel Grove—a neighboring town—but they never believed her.

Until she would say, "Have you ever looked at a newborn baby? How they never look at you but around you? It's because you're not their mother and they don't trust you, and are judging you by your aura."

That always shut them up. Carmen accepted her life as a Holie, but never embraced it the way she was supposed to. Carmen believed that the best way to live your life was as a Holie and a Gunner simultaneously. To use your judgment to bend the rules without breaking them. It worked well for her. She was more positively grounded than any of them, even their father, Grayson.

Salt licked at the sand beneath the flip flops Jett had made for herself. Beyond the shore, waves leapt intermittently towards the dark sky. No one went to the beach for pleasure anymore. She couldn't remember the last time she'd seen a child. She could imagine one, playing in the water at the shore, but it would just hurt her. She ignored the wish until it went away, overturned by something—someone—else.

Jett felt *him* before she saw him. So did Chris; his energy beside her spiked just as she turned her head to look at the unknown man. It took some practice to efficiently read the energy of one she had just met, but she would never have that problem with Chris, her best friend (other than her sister, but that hardly counted). Chris's energy practically belonged to her, and vice versa. They'd been side by side like this for years. If it were fear he was feeling, her heart would pound. But it didn't. It felt more electric than damaged.

Chris was intrigued, and so was Jett.

The man stood at the edge of a now battered and cracked highway people used to call PCH. The tattoos that weaved and knotted into one another trailed from his wrists, up his arms, and disappeared under the black sleeves of his cotton t-shirt. The body art must have been from Prius. Her kind would never pierce the skin intentionally; preserving the body in its natural form was essential to life, and to death. The Gunners—a family this man, standing just feet away, most certainly belonged to—would, if they could find the supplies. (Not that there were any real supplies left from Prius.) And this man was definitely a Gunner.

Jett flipped the switch in her mind, releasing the intangible white light from around her body. She focused on him; what he would look like without eyes and skin and everything that made up his physical form. What he would feel like. His heart beating against hers. What color he would be if her eyes were a paintbrush and his brain were a canvas. She stared at the middle of his forehead, photographing every essence that floated in her peripheral vision. She read him. His energy hit her, and she tilted her head as if compelled. His soul embodied the form of something in between *them* and *us*. In fact, it was a lot closer to *us*.

He clearly wasn't *really* a Gunner, because he hadn't killed her yet, and he wasn't a Holie, obviously. She guessed that very fact made him a Holie. Because he couldn't be labeled or judged as one thing.

But, based on his appearance, he was a Gunner, not a Holie, and he didn't belong in that in-between. He didn't belong here. But he was. Here.

*   *   *

One hour before

Grayson's pace inadvertently slowed—not that he was typically a speed-walker in retrospect—as a rainbow of a creature up in a tree bloomed in his vision. The vibrant owl watched him as Grayson dug his bare feet into the dirt below. Grayson caught its transparent stare from the animal's ice-white eyes. Grayson didn't move. His fear of the owl was founded. He didn't wonder if it had the power to destroy him; he knew it did, and would. He only wondered how it would destroy him. His family: the Holies. The whole world. He was responsible for the Holies, and if he didn't survive, neither would they.

Grayson didn't abandon his persistent lock with the creature's eyes as a rough sound of crinkled paper drifted in the distance. In that moment, he didn't physically turn his back on the owl, even if his energy and his mind had.

A Gunner. Within a fifteen-foot radius. Just a young man.

No Holie would make a sound like that, not in these woods. Or in any woods. *But neither would a Gunner*, he thought. They were careless, not stupid.

The feral growl that filled the crevices of the forest confirmed his suspicions. Only an animal that ate humans would make a sound like that, and that's what Enders were. Flesh-eating animals. Zombies untrustworthy and broken by their own survival instincts.

The young man's heart beat harmlessly in Grayson's head, like a drum drowned out by a sea of gold far enough away that you could hear it before you could see it. The Gunner. He was alone. Armed, but alone, and not necessarily dangerous. Not to Grayson, anyway.

Though he strived to resist his own curiosity, for once, Grayson failed. His daughter, Jett, and Chris too, would be mortified. Disappointed, or confused, maybe. But contrary to popular belief, Grayson wasn't perfect, and there were no Holies here to judge him.

He spun his feet in the dirt that buried them so that he could see around the tree. Growling through breaths—or breathing with growls, he wasn't sure—was the Ender, an animal concoction of blood and saliva and sweat and flesh gooping from its teeth. A zombie. As a hunchback, it barely stood between the two trees that shielded Grayson, its flesh hanging off its bones and its ripped jeans hanging off its waist.

As Grayson sensed the creature, it was obvious that the creature sensed him too—albeit by a different method—based on the depth of its growl intensifying and the mechanical shift of his feet in an attempt to gain on him, like some kind of dancing robot. It was the nature of their existence. Slow, stupid, and ugly, but lethal.

Grayson waited.

This young man wasn't like the others, but Grayson definitely hadn't expected the serene quality that enveloped the Gunner in the moment. He wasn't sure what he expected of the Gunner—he hadn't come in contact with one for some time—but definitely not that. Maybe some kind of running karate kick or something.

Tattoos crawling up his arms and into the sleeves of his t-shirt, his cropped haircut beckoning his poor excuse for a five-o'clock-shadow, the young man calmly walked up to the Ender, elbowed it hard in the jaw, and stabbed it in the heart with a hunting knife.

All the movies from Prius were a poor excuse for realistic science-fiction; the notion that a zombie had to be permanently killed via the brain was ridiculous at best. Zombies were living things before they were zombies, and so were Enders. Living things. They could be killed like anything else with a heart: by brute force.

From the blow to its jaw or the knife wound in its heart, or both, the Ender dropped like an overweight sack, and the young man retrieved his knife, cleaning it on his jeans before holstering it.

The Gunner wasn't a boy or even a very young man, really. To Grayson, an old man who had survived an apocalypse (so far) with two grown children, the Gunner was a boy. But he wasn't a boy just like Grayson's daughters weren't girls. The Gunner was a handsome man in his early twenties.

"Th—" Grayson covered his mouth and coughed into his hand, clearing his throat. He hadn't spoken out loud to himself in months. To someone else? Years. His people— the Holies—they didn't speak.

Well, they weren't supposed to.

"Thank you," he said eventually, his voice untrustworthy and broken like the existence of the Ender dead on the ground beside his feet.

The Gunner straightened his back self-consciously. Most men were no match for Grayson's intimidating six-foot-four-height, and neither was the Gunner. Grayson stepped back to help him feel at ease.

"I thought you Holies don't talk," the Gunner accused.

Grayson laughed, a sound that escaped from deep within his core. "My daughter never stops talking. But no, the rest of us don't talk much. Not unless we have to."

The Gunner sunk his hands into his pockets. Grayson looked up at the tree, now void of the owl. "What's your name?"

"Devlin Shea," he said, and then, "you cannot stay here." The Gunner felt the need to inform him this while eyeing him from gray beard to bare feet. "More will come."

"We'll be fine. My family is very resourceful. But thank you for your concern."

The Gunner seemed to be confused by his own existence. He looked down, looked up, nodded, turned, turned back, opened his mouth, closed it, and left. A tortured young soul, like Grayson's daughter, Jett. Grayson watched the Gunner disappear into the trees, knowing full well that he couldn't save his soul. No human could save another; they could only save themselves.

Grayson sat and watched the stillness that was the Ender's failed attempt at life. Beside him lay a leaf, lost in the seasons of a backwards world. The leaf, its yellow stem broken from its body, bled its life, dying its own edges with its insides. What was left of the yellow-green, living thing, was now caked with decay so black that not even the rain could wash it away, and all that was left was black and red. Pain overruled by evil.

The sound hadn't been paper but that of the leaf, its life poisoned by the death that stomped on it. In this world, the dead things killed the living things as punishment for the living things and their need to kill other living things.

Or maybe the universe was just an asshole.

CHAPTER 2

"HI," THE MAN WAVED AS HE STEPPED closer to Jett and Chris.

Jett leaned forward, as if through physical exertion she could make herself say something, but nothing came out. She wasn't sure how her voice would sound if it did. She couldn't remember the last time she'd spoken. A month, two, at least.

Jett's world turned tranquil when the sound of Chris's voice drifted into the morning air. She hadn't heard it in a while, either.

"You might want to chill...for a minute," Chris said, holding up his rough, weathered hand.

The man halted.

"You guys are Holies, right?" he asked breathlessly, like he'd been running or something. "I mean, obviously, you guys are Holies...right?"

Chris nodded apprehensively, somewhat self-consciously looking down at his hippy-ish clothing.

"So you won't hurt me," the Gunner said rather than asked.

"Not unless provoked," Jett said.

The loaded threat she had intended rang flat. Her voice sounded like shattering glass. It was exactly as she was afraid; she sounded like a twelve-year-old boy. *Use it or lose it,* Carmen's voice bounced around her head.

I'll take my chances, Jett thought, banishing the thought of her sister from her mind.

"Well, I don't have my gun on me, so…" The man hesitated as he waited for a reply from either of the Holies. When nothing came, he resumed his approach through the sand until he was arms-length away. He half-smiled, not bothering to offer his hand like people once did. "Devlin Shea."

He had beautiful eyes. Large eyes the color of the ocean, so endless Jett could swim in them for days. The rest of him was unremarkable, though. Nothing like Chris's defined features and smooth skin. This man couldn't pass for a Holie if his life depended on it. He looked to be nothing more than a soldier in need of a shave. But it didn't matter. If it came down to it, he'd be welcomed anyway, if determined unthreatening. A determination Jett and Chris had already made the moment they read him. That's what it meant to be a Holie.

Jett was suddenly ashamed of her outburst. Grayson would be mortified.

"Victoria Jetilyn Fournier," she said finally, accenting her French heritage with the surname. "Jett. And this is Christopher Reed."

"Do you guys stay…" the Gunner looped his finger in the air, "…around here, somewhere?"

"Here, sometimes," Jett said, "at the beach. But yes. Our family has a camp across the road. Which we should probably be getting back to, shortly."

"Well," the Gunner ran his hand over his cropped black hair, clearly disappointed at her curtness. "It was nice meeting you."

Jett noted his lack of ambition or persistence where it concerned some kind of potential friendship with a couple of Holies. He was different, but he wasn't stupid like the rest of them. His mind was open, and Jett liked what she could feel of him.

"Yeah, man, you too," Chris said. He lightly and absent-mindedly took hold of her hand and began leading her up the sand hill to the highway above.

"Hey, Jett?" Devlin called behind her.

She hesitated on her feet before she turned around.

"There are Enders in those woods."

"No there aren't," she assured him.

"Yes." He was adamant. "There *are.*"

"How do you know that?"

"Because I just killed one."

Jett watched him. Not him the man but *him.* What was within. It was the same. A mild in-between that intrigued her. He was aware of his own energy and he wasn't lying. His aura was calm, and so was his heart, his head, all of it. And if he were lying, he was a really, really good liar.

"Thank you," she said eventually.

Chris placed his hand upon the small of Jett's back, and they continued across the desolate highway.

"Nice guy," Chris whispered, his voice fading away along with the requirement to use it.

Jett shrugged. "He talks too much."

* * *

Chris thought it strange that Jett had referred to their place as their 'camp.' He didn't know what else she should've called it—their woods? Their Site of Living?—but it definitely wasn't a camp. Camps usually had things like tents and food and supplies; this group had blankets. Some knives. And dirt.

A few Holies lay on the ground between the trees, directly on the dirt, while others silently busied themselves with morning activities like collecting berries and assorted edible plants or sharpening knives and various other home-made weapons for the day's hunt. Their 'tribe' was small: fifteen, twenty tops. An essential number in order to run, or fight. If necessary.

Nobody spoke.

It was easier for Chris to admit he'd enjoyed speaking than it would be for Jett. He knew she'd enjoyed the change of pace—an actual conversation rather than just a connec-tion, but he wasn't sure if she'd ever admit it. Chris could say openly that he did in fact enjoy it, and nobody would blame him. They'd been Holies their whole lives, but he was still new to the Holie game. Even in Prius he'd been homeless; he survived, organic or not. Though the apoca-lypse was just a few years old, Jett and Carmen had been brought up this way, despite the no-speaking 'rule.'

That is, until Jett saved his life.

It'd been at least a month, maybe two since Jett had spoken a word out loud. It was, "please don't do that" or, "you just ruined everything," or something along those lines.

Silence had worked well for them. So far.

Though it did get quiet, sometimes.

Except when Carmen was around.

"Chris-TOE-ferrrrrr," Carmen sang, skipping over the younger Holies still sleeping on the ground in a small clear-ing in the woods, grasping his hand and spinning herself around him in a dance .

Chris kissed her cheek.

Carmen was certainly the more beautiful and more eccentric sister. Her honey brown hair exploded every morning to a mild frizz in the beach air. She had wide lips, a tiny nose, and huge hazel eyes. Even in rags and a tat-tered sweater, three years after the last bottle of foundation had been manufactured, she was one of the most beautiful women any man had ever seen.

But Chris didn't love her. Which was why he kissed her cheek, and not the center of her forehead where the pineal gland was located. Which was why he didn't kiss her where he might have kissed her sister. But that was way over, now. He'd ruined it. By kissing Jett that one time on The Nowhere Train.

The sisters together though, were a sight for every pair of sore eyes that ever existed. Chris could remember just what the sun had once looked like when he laid his eyes upon Jett and Carmen, voicelessly conversing with one another. Soon he forgot all about Carmen, though. He could see Jett's legs through the white lacy dress she'd made from the material he'd found for her. He'd take everything he said back for just one more night alone on the beach with her. To tug on her blonde hair—for that he'd trade every spoken word he would say for the rest of his life.

But he wasn't going to get it. Not in this lifetime. Maybe the world was backwards, like Carmen said. It had to be, for the way he was feeling right now.

"Boyd!" Carmen wailed suddenly.

From the dirt, like an overactive blossom, popped a dark, shaggy head as Boyd Williamsen awoke. Boyd's family and Jett's were neighbors and they grew up together, eventually leading to his relationship with Carmen.

"Yeah, babe," he grunted, rubbing at his head over the bright headband that Jett had probably also made.

Boyd still had sunglasses on from the night before, and probably four days before that.

"Eamus," Carmen commanded. *Let's go.*

Chris looked up from Jett at another approach. As naturally beautiful as Carmen was, Dama Booker had the kind of beauty that would once have belonged in a magazine or on a runway. Five-foot-eleven with cropped black hair and smooth skin, she was an exotic sort of young woman who had the body of a Parisian model. She wore cutoff jeans and some tight top she'd found, a very Dama-like outfit that showed off her long limbs. It shouldn't have mattered what they looked like in this world, but it did, to them. And Chris and Boyd noticed.

Dama hugged Chris. It wasn't one of those lame side hugs that he used to give girls in high school, but a real embrace. Holies didn't believe in that fake shit.

Dama, along with Boyd, grew up with Jett and knew a lot more of Jett (and Chris) than Carmen did. He guessed that she knew he needed the hug.

Jett's glare at Chris demanded his presence. He flipped the switch and let her in. He read her. His chest warmed as his heart began to beat a deep rhythm like the sound coming from a hand drum on a Venice boardwalk corner.

They were both purposely lagging. They really, really just didn't want to deal with the idea of moving. Not again. And again. And again. Maybe, like a bunch of immature twenty year olds, they could just be stupid for a while.

But he hadn't forgotten what Devlin had said.

Because I just killed one.

They hadn't seen an Ender in weeks. If they had, they wouldn't have stayed there.

Chris nodded. Grayson. They needed to talk to Grayson.

CHAPTER 3

HANDS ENTWINED, CHRIS AND JETT WEAVED through the trees of Malibu Creek, following the unmasked trail of serenity that Grayson's peaceful energy left behind. Chris allowed himself to think of the Gunner as they walked. He realized it more than likely appeared to Devlin that Jett was Chris's girlfriend. Their tendency to embrace human contact—her hand in his, his fingertips on her lower back—would give the wrong impression to someone who wasn't a Holie.

That was not Chris's intention. In fact, he had no intention at all. Chris and Jett had done what they had done for so long, that his behavior with her was so natural. And even if they weren't—if he were with Dama or Carmen—the outcome would be the same. There was no harm in human contact in their world. No shame in it. Unlike those in Prius that masked it. People like the Gunners.

He did feel shame, though, that he may have inadvertently messed that up for her. There was...something between them, obviously.

"Stop," Jett spoke unexpectedly, and her voice vibrated loudly in his ears.

She pressed her lips together like she regretted it, like she didn't mean to open her mouth. It was like once she'd spoken with Devlin, after months of silence, she couldn't stop.

"Stop being so negative," she said so quietly that he barely heard her. "I don't want to block you out right now."

Chris didn't reply.

They halted as Grayson came into view. He had his head tilted up to the sky. On a tree branch before him perched an owl, its feathers vibrant against the grayish sky. Blues and greens and reds, a contrast against its wide white eyes, like Devlin's. It stared into the distance.

Jett was not a fan of owls. She said they were creatures of the underworld, and if you saw one, someone close to you would die. This belief was, of course, contrary to all the myths surrounding owls that had existed in Prius.

Grayson sighed and slowly turned around. His reaction to the creature was as if he shared his eldest daughter's insights. Grayson looked like Hemingway, just less... drunk. His beard surrounded his smile like the snow would a pale cottage in the middle of a winter wonderland. His vibrant green eyes invited them to show him why they were there. Jett had once told Chris that Grayson's eyes hadn't always been like that. That when he created the Holie way of life, his eyes had changed color from dull to luminous. This was what happened when you embraced the energy that most humans refuse to believe exists.

Chris released Jett's hand, but as he stepped back to let them communicate, Grayson spoke in a deep drawl that Chris had never heard before that moment.

"I saw him," Grayson said quietly. "The Gunner. I saw him take down the Ender."

"Where?" Jett asked frantically.

"Not far from here."

"What do you want us to do, Dad?"

Nothing else was spoken. And, per Grayson's explicit, wordless instructions, that's exactly what they would do. Nothing. Because Grayson didn't want to scare the shit out of everyone for one Ender.

Which was fine. Jett liked the beach. Even if it did have zombies running across it every so often.

* * *

Jett and Chris met Carmen, Boyd, and Dama at the edge of the woods. Jett traded Chris's hand for Dama's as they crossed PCH back to the sand and beach. Carmen was running her mouth endlessly to Boyd like a child whose mother was too busy to entertain her stories, until Jett cut her off.

"Carmen, please...stop talking," Jett said quietly.

Chris imagined Carmen clenching her lips shut at Jett's reprimanding tone—whenever Jett spoke, Carmen listened—but when he looked at Carmen, he found her mouth gaping open. Chris followed her gaze to the edge of the shore. There, he saw the Gunner sitting on the sand, his back to them. Devlin. Carmen smiled widely, skipping over to him, but Jett's arm across Carmen's chest halted her.

They stared at one another and shared an intimate moment between sisters.

"So, what?" Carmen asked.

Jett sighed and walked ahead of their group to approach. Devlin looked over his shoulder at her.

"Do you smoke?" she asked hesitantly.

"Cigarettes?" he asked, his face crinkling into his own confusion. They didn't exactly look like the smoker type.

"What? No," Jett answered incredulously, as if the mere thought of it was absolutely ridiculous. "Herb."

"Do I smoke weed?" Devlin laughed. It was a deep, throaty sound Chris hadn't heard in a very, very long time. "Not in a while. But I'm down."

"You're um, welcome. To join us," Jett stuttered. She held out her hand to help him up.

He took it, and the six of them—the Holies, and one Gunner—smoked a joint.

*　*　*

"Why are you still here?"

Jett lay in the loosely packed sand, the gray sky watching from above. She could see only blackness from the inside of her eyelids. From somewhere behind her, Chris's energy beat in her chest like an old heart with barely a will to survive after its stretched years. Like alcohol, marijuana intensified the effects of energy work, albeit in a different way. It slowed the background noise of the world so that she could focus on just one thing at a time. But it wasn't because she was high. Chris—and his energy—was like that. Calmer than any being she had come in contact with on this earth, calmer, even, than her father. It's why Chris was her best friend. He kept her grounded. And she kept him flying.

Jett felt Devlin's energy shift from beside her, from void to aware. His blue eyes were looking at her; she could feel them on her skin, warm, as if they were the sun and not eyes.

Jett didn't open her eyes.

"I often wonder that myself." Devlin's voice came out slow and calculated, as if he chose his words carefully. "Where this will to survive comes from in a world that isn't worth surviving anyway. Why we don't just let them eat us, or, better yet, shoot ourselves in the fucking head. Sorry." Devlin cleared his throat.

Jett failed to hold in the laugh that escaped her, but didn't fail to notice Chris's energy perk up behind her when it happened. She laughed at more than one thing in that moment, but she didn't know what was more influential: the fact that Devlin felt the need to apologize for dropping an f-bomb, or his apparent need to explain in depth the way of the world when she had silently meant *what are you still doing here* as in *why are you still on the beach.*

It was too late for humor, though, in a moment when her eyes were now open and watching Devlin look at her like she was an unappreciative bitch.

"I'm sorry," she said, faintly smiling at him. "I meant, what are you doing here, you know, as in this...general location."

Devlin covered his face with his hands and laughed for a long time. "I didn't want to go home," he mumbled eventually.

This conversation was like a mentally ill patient with bipolar disorder. As the air around them went from deep to frivolous, it was unstable and it was untrustworthy and it was... exhilarating.

"That sounds awful," Jett said. "Not having anyone you particularly want to go back to."

Devlin shrugged his shoulders against the soft sand. "I don't have to go back, I guess. But I always do."

"Why?"

His stare into her eyes was intense. "I don't know."

*   *   *

Devlin looked on his family's camp from the top of a sandy hill, slicing from an apple he retrieved from some probably forbidden, i.e. poisoned, tree and tossing the pieces in his mouth. He realized what he was doing as he folded the knife. Not the same one he killed the Ender with earlier; there were worse ways to die, like from a poisoned apple. He wasn't a Neanderthal, as far as he was aware, and was perfectly capable of eating an apple like a normal human being by taking a bite out of it, even if there weren't any normal human beings around.

He chucked the stupid apple behind him in an effort to silence his inner ranting. Surely he could avoid thinking of that girl, Jett, by some means more intellectually valid than eating a fucking apple.

She'd gotten in his head; of that he was sure. He'd felt her presence caress his mind as he approached her. Like the rest of the Gunners, he'd known of, or heard of, the Holies' power on a physical level, but that didn't make it right. It broke some kind of personal space rule, right? Digging into someone's body without their permission?

That was why he, as a Gunner, was supposed to hate her.

Which was an idiotic thing to believe, obviously. Or maybe not. Hippies and Conservatives had been at war in Prius, so it made sense that Holies and Gunners would be at war now, even if there was no sense in being at war in the first place.

Devlin's camp was not a sight for sore eyes, as the expression went in Prius. It looked like fucking Waterworld without the water. Materials made for pirates, such as nets and canvas overhangs, were collected to create makeshift forts. They littered the camp like half-assed teepees only the white man would take credit for; Devlin wished for one of those Disney Princess sheets to liven up the place a bit. Not to mention the guns stacked on top of each other in three-foot-high towers of steel and wood just outside each tent. Seventeen people did not need that many firearms; they couldn't even carry them all, let alone fire them all. They had enough ammo to survive three apocalypses, probably.

But that was Robert Shea, King of survival, King of these Gunners. King of everything, including Devlin's life. Father. Rather than step into the fortress of war, Devlin would rather back away from this hill and run. He probably would, too, if Shea hadn't already seen him.

Devlin stomped down the hill in his combat boots, straightening his shoulders and flattening his face into an expressionless transparency that everyone would look straight through. Everyone but Shea.

"Good morning, sir." Devlin approached the man who looked to be a forty-year-old version of himself, Shea's feet cropped together and his arms stiff at his sides.

"Devlin, son," Shea said. "Where'd you run off to?"

"Scoping. Took down an Ender."

"Where?"

"East." *South.* "About four miles." *Two.*

"Anything else?"

"No, sir."

"I don't see the necessity in jumping ship if it was just one."

"10-4."

Devlin's father nodded, taking in the stubble on Devlin's face. "Go get yourself cleaned up, son."

"Yes, sir."

CHAPTER 4

JETT CAME TO, GROUNDED by an aura of warmth. Chris had always been that way: unnaturally warm. If you asked him, he'd say he was always hot, but to Jett, he was... he was Chris. He felt like a bed felt when you hadn't slept in three days, the blanket stuck in your armpits and the fan making that gentle hum that would put you to sleep like your mother's voice would when you were little.

He felt like home.

Jett squeezed his fingers before running the tips of hers up his forearm.

He made a sleepy noise, a muffled groan. He was out. He wouldn't wake up anytime soon; Chris slept like the dead. Jett probably should've laughed at the irony of that in the midst of a zombie apocalypse, she thought, but she didn't.

Jett rolled out of Chris's arms and found the stars above, clouded by the vomit of the dead in the sky. She didn't know what time it was, but it wasn't the *right* time for her father to be pacing between the trees.

It was never the right time for that.

Jett silently stood up from the cushion of the dirt below, and went to her father. He saw her, halted, and sat down directly in front of her. Accepting his wordless invitation, she sat next to him, and they lay back in the dirt, gazing at the kiss between the tops of the trees and the dirty sky.

"We're leaving," said the voice that Jett barely knew next to her ear.

Jett opened her eyes, not really remembering when she'd closed them. It was so easy to fall into the energy of someone close, someone you knew and loved, and forget who you were just for a moment. Because they all wanted the same thing.

Nothing. They wanted nothing.

Jett turned her head to meet her father's eyes.

"Why are you talking?" she said quietly so she wouldn't wake anyone up to the reality that Grayson was speaking aloud.

"Because you want to talk."

"That wasn't a good enough reason for you to speak to me when I was a child."

"As a father, it is my job to raise you into a beautiful human being in a way that I see fit. It is also my job to trust you to make good decisions as an adult. I have succeeded in both. You have achieved both."

Jett stared at him. She was not a master compliment-taker. For obvious reasons. "Do we really have to run from them *all* the time, Grayson?"

Neither she, nor anyone in her family, found it strange that she called her father Grayson. Partly because Jett rarely ever spoke except to her sister in secret and occasionally to Chris—occasionally as in, every couple months—but mostly because she had never called him Dad in the first place. She didn't really need to call him anything. He was a man who raised her, whom she loved and looked up to. But, while they were talking, she had to call him something.

An electric feeling tickled her core, shooting a blue glow through her skin. Devlin.

"It doesn't have anything to do with him," Jett said, responding to the question his energy had just posed to her soul. "It has to do with us. We can't run from them for the rest of our lives."

"What would you have us do, Jetilyn?" Grayson asked her in a calm whisper. "Kill them? Kill them all?"

Jett closed her eyes and hesitantly shook her head, losing the battle she never wanted to fight against her father. "When?"

"Two days."

As she got up and disappeared into the trees, Jett caught sight of Chris's eyes, watching and listening to the conversation play out between father and daughter.

Chris was more like the dead than she originally thought. Awake and hungry.

CHAPTER 5

DEVLIN WOKE UP ALONE. Not that he would wake up any other way on any other given day, but the rest of his camp wouldn't. Those who didn't have a family would tent with other members of the camp to save space. And less tents to carry with them. Devlin guessed there were some perks to being the King's son, getting a tent of his own. All he knew was he definitely wasn't sleeping with that asshole.

Devlin didn't really know why he hated his dad so much, other than the fact that Shea was a dick. He guessed that was a good enough reason.

Devlin didn't understand why their lives had to be led by war, and Robert didn't understand why Devlin couldn't understand why that was the way it had to be. There was no reason why Devlin couldn't understand; he was given his first rifle at six years old; he was sent to Boot Camp instead of Boy Scouts.

Devlin was accepted into the Army at a younger age than should have been legal because of the outstanding defense Robert had fought for his country in Desert Storm and in Vietnam. He went on to achieve Green Beret status at the youngest age in history, at seventeen years old. He'd been known to unofficially lead unconventional warfare missions where he was stationed in Afghanistan due to his outstanding skills, unstoppable drive, and military heritage. That was right before he got out, at nineteen, when the Enders began to rise out of the ground like fucking sunflowers. The first one rose in Southern California, not far from where they were now. Devlin wasn't exactly sure how the zombies got their name, but it made sense. They ended life in a physical sense, and they were ending life as the living had always known it. Every day. That life would never be the same for any person who had survived this apocalypse, and they would all die eventually. Probably from an Ender bite.

Having been through all of that, Devlin still didn't understand war. He only did it because it was expected of him. Taught to him. Drilled into him. It was who he was; he just didn't know why.

Devlin had told Jett that he didn't know why he always went back to his camp, but that was a blatant lie. He went back because he didn't feel he had another choice. There was only one man Devlin knew who was more successful at Search and Rescue than himself: Robert Shea.

If Devlin didn't come back, Shea would find him. Shea would *always* find him. Devlin had lied to Jett in that moment because he was ashamed of his family, of his life. He didn't doubt that the Holie man he'd run into in the woods was considered family by Jett, but he was almost positive it was more than that. The old man looked like her. She had an old soul that shone through her eyes, like the man did.

He was probably her father.

Devlin rolled out of his winter-rated sleeping bag, which he slept in naked on instinct to avoid hypothermia. Not that he would there, or anywhere anymore. The rise of the Enders snowballed the longest and most intense global warming event ever. There was a geographical area near here that was once known for its rain because it was smack dab in a pocket in Southern California, but they didn't get that anymore. He couldn't remember the last time he had smelt the natural scent of rain.

Dressed, he emerged to find the clouds hovering over the trees, barely lit by the distant sun. It was hot, but it was dark. He couldn't remember the last time he was able to get lost in a sunset, either. Sometime in Prius, maybe.

His boots stomped towards the hill that he'd come in from the evening before, but a stern "Halt" did exactly what it was supposed to.

Devlin stopped and slowly turned around.

His father waited for an explanation. He wouldn't wait long, though.

"Perimeter." Devlin smiled the mischievous grin that his father usually wore at the mere thought of battle. "And beyond. Just in case."

Shea's expression bended into a grin that matched his son's, a sparkle in his eyes that terrified Devlin.

"Before seventeen-hundred hours. I would like to speak with you."

"Yes, sir." Devlin didn't salute his father, but he might as well have. "Seventeen-hundred hours."

He wouldn't need that much time to get back to the beach, but he'd take it anyway. Or he'd try.

* * *

Chris was an orphan.

Well, not really. When he'd lost his parents—to the Enders, Jett found out much later —Chris was seventeen.

There weren't enough Enders back then for anyone to really notice—a few here and there throughout the country—and Chris wasn't comfortable talking about his parents back then. He wasn't exactly comfortable talking about them now, or any of his family for that matter, but he did eventually tell her what happened.

Jett never pushed him, but they eventually built a friendship based on trust, and Chris just...told her. They'd been watching a movie on Jett's couch long before the Enders were actually an apocalyptic problem and there was still power. Chris's admission of how he came to be the homeless boy holing up in the abandoned house across the street from Jett's inevitably led to her family's discovery of the origins, and the cause, of the apocalypse. Why the dead were rising.

The four Fourniers—Jett, Carmen, Grayson, and Amy—made a pact, in order to protect Chris, that they would never tell the real story to a soul outside of their family, and as far as Jett knew, they hadn't. It made them the only people on Earth who knew why this horrible monstrosity had happened—not that it was necessarily useful. It didn't help them stop it. The only way to stop it was to kill them all. They had all killed since Prius, all the Holies, but only when they had to. They mostly just let the Gunners do the dirty work and tried not to get in the Gunners way so they weren't murdered themselves. The Gunners were killers; that's what they did. That's all they were.

When Jett found Chris, he refused to speak to her—or anyone, really—which made it very easy for Jett to teach him the ways of her family and her community. He already knew how to use his energy, so he was accepted into their way of life and into their family immediately. Jett didn't even have to ask Grayson to take Chris into his home as one of his children; Grayson did it right away, and of his own accord.

Grayson would be mortified by what Jett had done to Chris four years after that day she found him shaking in that abandoned house. It was just two months ago now, when she made him feel like an alien and that everything different about him was all his fault, as if he didn't feel enough of that already. Grayson would likely disown his eldest daughter. Throw her out and leave her to die. The world knows she would've deserved it.

The moment that Chris kissed Jett in The Nowhere Train, she revolted against him. She hit him and called him a monster and he stayed. He stayed by her side like he always had, because he was a good person, and she was an asshole.

The universe requires balance.

Jett ignored the stomping noise next to her head, the packed sand masking it into a gentle tap. She only honed in on the electric energy trickling through the air above her head until it lay down next to her. She opened her eyes to find Devlin staring sideways at her.

Her heart beat her confusion into his head, in an effort to ask him *what* he was exactly, but in the same moment that she remembered Devlin didn't know how to communicate that way, with energy, he said aloud to her, "Did you sleep out here? By yourself?"

"No," she heard herself whisper, and she cleared her throat to make her voice come out like she did actually know how to use it. "No, I didn't—not that I wouldn't be able to take care of myself—but, no, I didn't really sleep at all."

"Do you have trouble sleeping?" Devlin asked.

"No. But my father was up, so I was up."

"You two are close?"

"We used to be. I mean, yeah, I guess. But no one is really close with my father anymore. Or he's not close with anyone else. Not since my mother died."

"Ender?" Devlin coughed awkwardly. "I mean, if you don't mind me asking."

"No. I don't mind. And, yes. An Ender chewed her face off."

"That's terrible. My mother died in childbirth, so I have no idea what that's like. To have a mother, or to lose her. It must have been very hard on you and your family. I'm sorry."

Jett stared at him in bafflement, again wondering who—and what—the hell this guy was.

"Do you want to have breakfast?" Jett blurted.

"Breakfast," Devlin snickered, his frosty eyes smiling with it. "You guys are...vegan, I guess?"

"Yes," Jett said sarcastically. "You know, grass and berries and shit."

Devlin dug his face into the sand and laughed. "You don't speak like a hippie like, at all."

"Yeah well, neither do you. Are you going to make me drop and give you twenty or something?"

Devlin flashed a smile for her benefit, but it wasn't the same. She'd touched a nerve by referencing the Gunners yet again, but she still didn't know why.

"Come on," Jett said, touching his arm and standing up, "I'll show you a river dance."

Devlin followed, laughing. "Are you serious?"

"No. Definitely not."

* * *

Aside from what they wore and what they carried, the Holies weren't really that different from the Gunners. The Holies had a camp, though it was void of any equipment. Devlin couldn't recall if Jett had at any time called it a *camp* or if he'd just referred to it as such in his own mind.

Jett's family, as she called them—Devlin was sure of that much at least—sat as a haphazard group of tunics and sandals scattered between the trees. A few blankets lay here and there, accompanied by some canteens that weren't made from metal or plastic, but some hard, cloth-like material. The girl with Jett's tiny nose sat propped against a tree trunk, a very hipster-ish looking man lying with his head in her lap. From this distance, she appeared to be eating freshly-picked spinach from her hand.

Devlin would have shouted at her, slapping the vegetables from her hand, if he hadn't caught three more not-undead people near her eating the same thing.

He looked to Jett who stood next to him, smiling up at him. He thought about the canned food and scraps of non-perishables that he and his Gunners could get their hands on.

"You're *growing* food?" He asked incredulously. "I mean, I know things grow still, but how are you eating it and not *dying*, or worse?"

"Whatever do you mean?" Jett asked.

"The Enders, Jett. They die, and they bleed into the soil. You are essentially *eating* them."

The smile sagged off her face like she was a dying old woman.

"You'd have to talk to Chris about that," she said quietly, looking down and leading him to her sister.

Pretending to ignore Jett as she stepped away from him and towards Chris, he stared dumbfounded at Carmen as she offered her handful of spinach to him.

She rolled her eyes at him in the most dramatic way he had ever seen.

"Chris!" Carmen called out, oblivious to the exchange of tension occurring in this very moment.

Jett glared with the force of a thousand knives at Carmen.

Carmen ignored her.

"Christopher, sit down," she said calmly. "We can't let him starve, for fuck's sake."

Chris did what was asked of him, leading Jett by her hand. The art of the poker face had been literally beaten into Devlin growing up, so it was unlikely that Jett would ever know how much her relationship with Chris was beginning to get under his skin. Then again, she could read him like no one else he knew could—facial expressions aside—so she might know already. It's not as if he had any claim on her, but he just wished he knew what was up with them. If they weren't together, then why did they appear to be? He just wished he knew because she was fucking beautiful and he wanted her and he didn't really have a lot of time, because zombies.

The five of them—Boyd, Carmen, Chris, Jett, and Devlin—sat in a circle that was quite hippie-ish, considering the fact that their legs were crossed and the lot of them were dressed like they were going to Woodstock, and, while Carmen and Boyd ate, Chris spoke very quietly. Devlin didn't think it would do any good, with the unspeaking people and the eerie quiet of the woods, but it was worth a shot.

"They aren't fueled by disease," Chris whispered, hanging his head before staring straight into Devlin's eyes. "They're fueled by magic."

Devlin's eyes pin-balled around the camp, his demeanor utterly still, eventually saying, "Surely the rest of them know what you're telling me."

"Yes," Chris answered. "But if they knew I was telling *you*, some of them would kill me. Even if you are unlike any Gunner we've ever come across."

Jett, unmoving, said nothing.

"What does that even mean? Mag—"

"Nobody fucking move."

Abruptly, Chris stood, barricading Jett with his body as the monster of a voice Devlin knew all too well thundered through the trees.

Jett's father, Grayson, appeared from nowhere, standing his ground in front of the clearing. Despite Robert Shea's warning, all the Holies shifted behind their leader.

Devlin saw his father with an AR-15 strapped to his back and a Glock .45 dangling from his fingertips, four of his best dumbasses with guns flanking him.

"Peace," Grayson choked out, lifting his palms.

"You kidnap my son, and you ask me for peace?" Shea growled. "I will kill all of you."

Grayson said nothing. Grayson would protect Devlin — Devlin understood that now — or he'd try. But he would fail.

Devlin shot up in a standardly stiff fashion, stalking in front of Grayson and saluting his father. "Sir, let them go. Please."

"You stand *with* them?" Shea roared at Devlin. "Against me?"

"No, sir."

"They did this. *All of this*." Shea waved his pistol. "They brought these monsters upon us, monsters who have destroyed our lives, and you protect them against your own family?"

Devlin waited.

"Answer me."

"Run," Devlin said just loud enough for Jett to hear, and as swiftly as he killed the Ender in the woods, he un-holstered his Springfield 1911, and cracked his father over the head with it.

"Run!" he said again, and shots fired.

"No!" he heard Jett scream, as she was dragged away from him. He didn't take her for the abandoning type.

*　*　*

"He doesn't like it. Me and you."

Jett stared off the cliff of Reynan Beach as her father and the others decided where they were going.

"I didn't even think about it," Chris continued. "Touching you. It's become so normal for us. But I didn't mean to screw anything up for you."

"It doesn't matter now," Jett's voice cracked, wondering why they were suddenly talking so much. She rubbed her forehead with the palm of her hand. "He's probably dead now."

"I don't think so, Jett. He's his son."

"They're *Gunners*, Chris. Like them, your family has spent generations killing each other, but they are way worse."

Chris laughed. "I love you, Jetilyn Fournier, but you don't know what the fuck you're talking about."

Her soul turned blue in his chest. Though she couldn't project it in a physical form, it was still there. Seeping from her skin.

"You need to find a man like Elias," he said, looking up at the black sky.

She rolled her eyes. "Are we seriously talking about this right now?"

"We have to sometime," Chris said, sitting down on the cliff, letting his legs dangle. As he wished, she joined him. "If we're ever going to be like...friends."

"Is that what you want?"

"It's better than nothing."

Jett sighed. "Well. No offense to your family, but I could never date someone as finicky as Elias. He was way too understanding about your grandfather's relationship with his wife."

"And you think that a man who would be understanding about us would be *finicky*?"

The blue exploded beside him and darkened to black as she refused to answer him.

Jett was still in love with Christopher Reed, and she had no idea what to do about it. Because they belonged together, obviously, but she was confused about him and about why Devlin intrigued her so much and she had no idea what to do about it. Especially Christopher Reed.

Christian Reed, as he was once called, after his grandfather.

"We have to save him," Jett eventually said.

"I know."

CHAPTER 6

IT WAS ONE OF SHEA'S GOONS who shot at him—if Shea were going to kill his son he was going to do it his damn self—and the dumb motherfucker missed. He'd never be as accurate as Shea or Devlin, but the guy wasn't a bad shot. Devlin wasn't swift enough to dodge bullets, but, thanks to his father, he had the art of anticipation down, and Bryan—the guy who shot at him—was an idiot.

As Devlin had cracked his father in the head, Shea had done the same to Bryan after the gun went off. Again, if anyone were going to kill Devlin Shea, it was going to be the guy who made him.

"A word with my son," Shea said, after the Holie family dispersed and as the dumbass writhed in pain on the ground.

The other three dragged him away. Devlin bent his knees, squatting, hanging his head and dropping his gun on the ground between his feet. Devlin only hoped he wouldn't beg for mercy this time. He only hoped he wouldn't beg his father to kill him, because then he'd know he was weak. As if he didn't know already, by the way he had just begged him to let the Holies live.

"You know you're going to track them yourself," Shea said quietly. "You know you're going to lead me to them so I can fucking mow them down."

"Yes, sir," Devlin said, not daring to look up at his father.

"Get up, you worthless piece of shit."

Devlin did, knowing that Shea only wanted him up so he could knock him down. At least he used his fists and not the gun this time.

* * *

"No," Jett said to her father, quiet and unanimated, but very adamant. Grayson having taken Chris's spot on the cliff and not having said a word, Jett was sure her father had lost his damn mind.

Grayson stared at her in an effort to calm her with his crisp gaze. He cocked his head to the side, pleading with her.

"No, Dad." *Why couldn't she shut up?* "You're crazy."

He held her hands in his. "They won't ever look for us there. And if they do, they'll die."

"And we won't?"

"We have Chris," Grayson whispered.

Tears streamed down Jett's pale face. "They almost killed him once, Dad."

"Almost. I don't think they'll really kill him, though. I think...I think they're in there somewhere."

Jett tasted bile in her throat. "That is the stupidest thing you've ever said to me."

He squeezed her hands. "Hear me out."

Jett stared at the black ocean below, broken by the sadness escaping her.

"I don't mean the turned ones, Jetilyn. I mean the original ones. Christopher's parents and grandparents. They were very powerful. That power doesn't just go away."

Jett let the tears dry on her face before looking up at her father. "If he refuses to go back, I won't stand with you."

"I know, Jetilyn."

"You know *what*?"

"I know that you love him. And you know that I would never ask you to leave his side."

*   *   *

Everything hurt.

His spleen. His spleen hurt, if that were a thing.

Devlin lay on the soft dirt, outside of a tent. He just didn't care enough to crawl inside his tent. The goons dropped him there when they carried him back, and he didn't bother getting up. No one dared speak to him or even approach him. Even if he felt as if he could get up, he wouldn't, because if he got away, he wouldn't survive, not like this.

His skin was caked with bruises and his own blood—he guessed. He didn't exactly have a mirror, but everything felt tender. If they didn't smell him first, they'd most definitely see him moving slowly, providing he could move at all.

Devlin refused to think about how he was going to get himself—and Jett—out of this mess. His father wasn't going to make him track because he was a better tracker—Robert Shea was most definitely a better tracker than his son—but because Devlin had betrayed him. Because Shea was so intuitive there'd be no way for Devlin to lead him astray; Shea would be tracking as Devlin did. This little murderous adventure would be nothing but a lesson dealt from Shea to Devlin. He'd have to escape if he didn't want Jett to die.

Of course, his father would just find him.

Which left one option. Not exactly ideal, but not impossible.

Instead of plans to free himself of the mess, he wondered whether Jett's—friend?—Chris, were insane or...*insane*.

For six hours, Devlin had spun the word *magic* around in his head, and had come up with nothing but the possibility that the Enders were sparkling vampires, or something.

Which obviously proved his own insanity.

He had to get to Jett if only to find out what the ever-loving fuck was going on in their world; and the only way to do that was to lead the Gunners to her.

As much of a selfish asshole that made him.

* * *

With the color violet, Jett's soul showed him Jasmyn Lake.

Chris turned away from her and vomited whatever was in his stomach, and then some. Bent over, he wiped his mouth with the back of his hand, and looked back at her.

Jett's entire existence shook with fear for him. She couldn't breathe, but she'd never show him that. "He thinks we'll be safe there."

"Do you?"

"Not really."

A tornado of a breath whirled from his lips. He nodded.

She grabbed his hand, Carmen grabbed hers, Boyd hers, and with the rest of them, they trekked the long stretch of Lilian Highway.

* * *

The world was so quiet.

A lot of people had died, and more had been eaten. There was no music, no hum of car engines, no children squealing after each other. There weren't even any stars. Once upon a time, the stars would be so bright above this highway that it would seem there were more of them than there was sky. But it was just sky now. Black, dusty sky above the long road that split the dense woods from the endless ocean. As eerie as it was, it felt normal. It *was* normal. This was their world now.

Jett supposed that they should've stopped, what with the late hour, but they hadn't yet. She didn't really know why, hadn't really thought about it. All her energy was expended into forcing one foot in front of the other.

Her hand still in Chris's, her energy sparked alive when she heard the noise, but her body didn't. In this new world, Chris had taught her to be still, stoic even to those experiences that required her attention. He'd taught her to be fearless.

He was the best there was at that kind of thing.

The sound of the cotton swashing against her leg as she lifted her skirt crashed in her ears. As the others looked to Grayson, he looked to her, unsheathing the knife from the leather strap around her leg.

With sheer will of her third eye, Jett urged her father to go on without her. One shake of the head in return.

He was into arguing with her lately.

Carmen and Boyd silently stepped back to flank her and Chris, and Grayson lost the battle.

Jett hoped they would all win the war.

Grayson wordlessly gave the order, and, as practiced, in small groups of three or four, the Holies journeyed on. All except four of them.

Lilian Highway was a Pacific highway bordered on one side by beach and on the other by forest on a large hill. In Reynan, where Chris and Jett sat on the cliff to talk about his family and about her love life, Chris's grandmother Jane's family once resided. There was a big mansion on the top of a hill several miles down the road. The house was gone, but the memories weren't. Not even for Chris, who hadn't yet been born at the time.

It was the dense forest that likely housed the rustling noise, like an eager hand in an empty bag of potato chips.

Boyd nodded, accepting instructions from Chris, and there was nothing Carmen could do about it because she couldn't overpower Boyd; or anyone really.

Jett didn't look at her sister before she walked into the trees beside Chris.

CHAPTER 7

CHRIS DIDN'T THINK JETT was really afraid of anything. Except him.

It wasn't an unhealthy fearlessness, like Will Smith appeared to be in most of his films; Jetilyn Fournier wouldn't need therapy in a normal world that had things like therapists. She wouldn't need Jesus or a creative outlet. Jetilyn was fearless in that her life's game plan wasn't fueled by fear, but by a constructive desire to be free. And she was. Jetilyn was fucking free, and nothing could touch her. Which is why she was so fearless.

Sometimes, Chris envied her; sometimes, he hoped with all the energy of his soul that he could attain such freedom, but subconsciously he knew better. So he let her protect him. Even if he was in a much better position, physically, to protect himself, and protect her, he let her protect him, especially now.

Chris was unsure how Jane had stayed away from this place so long. Granted, it held more pain than beauty for her, but it was more beautiful than it was painful, it would seem to Chris.

He felt, in the way that his parents had transformed into cannibalistic creatures that tried to eat him years before, that being given up for adoption and left to fend for yourself at sixteen, as his grandmother had been in this place, wasn't that bad. They were more similar than Chris had ever realized growing up. Though she'd died when he was so young, she was in his mother like the scent a candle left long after it had burned out.

Like Jane Wildes, her grandson had been abandoned by seemingly normal parents, in order to be saved by unconventional circumstances. She would die all over again if she knew he'd been referring to her as his grandmother this whole time, even if that was what she actually was, because, when she'd lived, she'd been so afraid of getting old. She never had, though, in the life of the living. She never had grown old, until now.

Ignoring what was staring him right in the fucking face, Chris tilted his head up at the sky to imagine the ray of glitter that would be reflecting off the tips of the evergreens had the sun shone anymore. What he found was an infamous dark cloud just the length of the small circular clearing in the woods where they stood. Chris closed his eyes as the gentle raindrops began to patter onto his cheeks. As the drizzle evolved into a downpour like no rain this area had seen in years, Jett's hand should have shaken in his. But it didn't. For the first time since the night he kissed her in the woods six months before, Chris felt that Jett did not fear him.

Maybe he would protect her, after all. Just a little.

He opened his eyes to find her staring in awe at him with those wide eyes she adopted right before she was going to slap him, and in that moment he knew that everything would be okay.

The redheaded creature in front of them wasn't the stunning beauty she'd been in Prius, and her husband was definitely not the artist that every woman in California wanted to have sex with. His beefy bicep had a chunk taken out of it, the guts of his one-time strength hanging out. The ocean-blue eyes the Linden family had been known for were clouded over with a milky fog in his head, and Chris could see the man's jawbone through the half of his face that was no longer there.

Beside him, the woman's luminous eyes were sealed shut, and her hair had dulled to an orange that was reminiscent of the tweaker mother in that movie *Requiem for a Dream*. Her violet sundress was ripped at the bottom seam, the cloth fraying over her bruised leg.

With eyes that could not see, Jane and Elias Linden stared at their grandson. Chris wasn't sure if Jett could discern his tears from the drops of rain on his face, but it didn't really matter.

He tugged on her hand to keep her with him just a moment longer.

Though no sound came out, Chris heard his full name burst from the zombie woman's lips as they moved. In the moment that Jett choked on her own breath, his knees buckled, and everything went black.

* * *

"Shit," Boyd muttered, as Jett's soft energy exploded in his chest, turning his lungs black. "Stay here."

"Have you lost your fucking mind? She is my *sister*, Boyd."

"Dammit, Carmen." Boyd held her by the shoulders and shook her slightly. "Two seconds. *Two seconds*, and I'll have them out, I promise."

He disappeared into the trees, and Carmen, rolling her eyes, unsheathed a knife from beneath her skirt. Stay there, she did not.

Because fuck that.

*   *   *

Despite his facial hair covering most of it, the wind in the woods hurt Boyd's face. The wind that should've been impossible in this clearing. They were surrounded by a dense cluster of trees and mountains in the distance that should've shielded any kind of breeze getting in, let alone a storm reminiscent of a fucking tornado.

Jett looked like a witch, her blonde hair spiking to the sky as she stood protectively with her back to Chris's body lying on the soft ground. Across from her were two Enders, dead on the ground with at least ten somewhat-living ones ready to strike behind them.

Boyd set his hand softly on Jett's back, and glared into her soul with a force as concerned as it was terrified.

She shook her head, confirming that Chris hadn't been bit. Sans warning, Jett charged forward, sinking her knife into the top of an Ender's skull. Per Jett's explicit instructions when he'd been standing out on the highway with Carmen, he just watched her work while he guarded Chris. She moved nimbly like a girl in pink dancing shoes, her hair whipping a yellowish trail in the rain as she sliced open the neck of one and left an arm dangling from another.

Jett's eagerness lightened from black to gray in the pit of Boyd's stomach just as Carmen appeared beside him.

"No," Carmen said. "We are not leaving her."

"Get him out!" Jett wailed, as she crouched to send her blade through the heart of another Ender, as seven more descended on her.

Planning to ignore her, Boyd moved to step forward but halted in his tracks as light shone through the clearing from above. The rain stopped. Jett stepped back, looking up at the sky cracking with sunlight.

Immediately, as if Enders were vampires and not zombies, they started dropping like flies.

"How the fuck are you doing that?" Boyd yelled over the wind.

Jett shifted around slowly, glaring at him.

She wasn't doing it.

Why was the sun shining?

Boyd spun, zoning in on Chris's seemingly lifeless body. Against the wet dirt, muddying his fingertips, Chris's hands were twitching. His eyes. His chest.

Boyd looked up as the last Ender fell to the ground, and like the sudden death of a flickering light bulb, the wind went out.

On the ground, Chris was still, and everything that was dead was really fucking dead. Boyd hadn't even had to lift a finger because the sky had just saved his ass.

Any other girl would've collapsed right there into a puddle of her own misery, but Jett, her pale skin drenched in blood and rain water and mud, stalked right past them like an emotionless robot.

"Wake him up," she said, and walked away.

CHAPTER 8

"THERE'RE SOME OLD TRAIN TRACKS," Chris crackled out, sitting up in the dirt before the endless pile of dead bodies, and rubbing his face raw with his hands. "It runs parallel to Lilian. They cleared the edge of the woods for it years ago to bring traffic out from Hazel Grove. But, as you know, no one ever leaves Hazel Grove. The rail shut down years ago."

Hazel Grove was a party town in Gray County, set between Devonbrook and Jasmyn Lake, and it was true that no one ever left once they arrived.

"There is an abandoned train there. The Nowhere Train. Jett will be there."

"How does she even know about it?" Carmen asked, perplexed, having never heard of it herself.

"Because I used to take her there," Chris said.

* * *

"Mount up," Devlin shouted deeply, from the top of the hill that oversaw their camp. "We're on the move."

He looked at his father as their group darted off like mice after the biggest piece of cheese the eye ever could see. Artillery was loaded, tents rolled, and men lined up just like they were told.

"What's your beef?" he asked Shea quietly. He wasn't feeling brave, just defeated. His father was going to kill him anyway.

The scowl seemed to have permanently etched itself into Shea's eyebrows. "They're responsible for all of this, Devlin. For your mother's death. For destroying our family and our world."

"Why? Because they're different?"

"Because they're fucking unnatural. There's so much you don't know, and you betrayed me based on your own ignorance."

"Then tell me."

"They call them the Enchanters. They sacrificed the lives of billions for one Romeo and Juliet story."

"You're not making any sense right now. Like, none."

"My cousin Daniel told me everything before he tried to eat my face. But right now, you're on a need to know basis, and you do not need to know. You're the son of a Gunner. So get your fucking gun, shut your mouth, and follow your orders."

*   *   *

Half of the cold, gray, steel train leaned off the side of the tracks into the dirt. Just like Chris had explained, the tracks invaded the woods, cutting a clean line all the way to Gray County. Jett's blonde hair was barely visible through one of the dirty windows, but she was there. Just like Chris knew she would be.

Carmen moved ahead of the two boys, stalking into the train like her sister might.

"How's Carmen feeling?" Chris asked Boyd quietly.

"She's feeling like she's pregnant in the middle of a fucking apocalypse."

Chris didn't know how he was supposed to respond to that, so he didn't.

The guys boarded the dilapidated train, quietly scuffling down the aisle past Jett and Carmen in the front, settling in the back.

They sat with their backs to the train windows, face-to-face in the rear seats on either side of the dirt-crusted aisle, hiding from the sisters in the front.

"What happened out there?" Boyd whispered.

"They were my grandparents," Chris spat out without hesitation.

Boyd nodded slightly. "I'm sorry, but, uh, that's really not what we're talking about."

Jett appeared in the rear, Carmen, looking blue, tight on her heels. Boyd beckoned Carmen over and held her together while she buried her face into his neck.

"Jetilyn, I have known you my whole life, and I can't even deal with the fact that you've been keeping something from me."

"It wasn't my secret to tell." Her voice cracked as tears swam down her face. Boyd cringed as Jett started to cry. None of them had seen her cry more than maybe three times in her life.

Chris held out his hand, and Jett joined him on the cushioned bench seat across from Boyd and Carmen. He encouraged her openness with a kiss on the top of her head, which, for once, she didn't revolt against. Jett had been loyal to him since she saved his life in that abandoned house across the street from her childhood home, and this was the least he could do.

"Chris's family was like us, except the energy was in their blood. They didn't have to teach themselves to utilize it like we did. Unlike us, they had power that was dictated by the color of their auras, which never changed. Like all humans, the shades of their auras changed shades, but never physical color. But no humans could see the auras, not even Holies." Jett didn't hesitate to seek skepticism from Boyd or Carmen.

The Holies were Jett's people and they would never doubt her. She continued. "Each aura dictated the power associated with the element the family could control. Chris's father and *his* father could manipulate the earth. With an inner power, they could move dirt and trees. They could crack the roads with their eyes. Chris's mother's father, Elias Linden, could fashion fire from nothing. His uncle could bring the wind, and so on. There were other, less powerful elemental families as time went on. Rain, moon, sun, but the original four—Brooks, Hadley, Reed, Clarke—were the *Mothers,* or mother elements."

"And your mother?" Boyd asked Chris.

Chris felt the color drain from his face before it actually happened. "My mother was a Brooks. She had all the power."

"How?"

"The Brooks were the original family. They delegated one power to each family in case their bloodline ever died out. It never did, though."

"When did this start?" Boyd asked.

Carmen sat up, silent.

"Since Salem," Jett interjected. "The Salem Witch Trials were cover-ups for the real witches, called the Enchanters. But the universe demands balance, and no power as strong as theirs could come without a downside. A curse was placed on the young Enchanters by the Brooks elders to keep them in check. A Brooks woman, like Chris's mother, wouldn't be permitted to marry a Reed man, like Chris's father, for the rest of eternity."

Boyd sunk in his seat as he saw where this was going.

"Starting with Lila Brooks," Jett explained. "And Adam Reed and on, Reed men kept chasing after Brooks women. It was an inner battle that each side fought, but never won, until the Brooks woman would have an unexpected change of heart and would leave the Reed man heartbroken for another family. Brooks and Reeds never eloped. Some sort of force always stopped it before it could happen. Until Abby Linden and Evan Reed."

"Your parents?" Boyd asked Chris.

Chris nodded.

"The curse said that," Jett said, "should a Brooks woman ever marry a Reed man, the powers would be stripped, and the Enchanters would cease to pass on their gift to their children. Except when Abby and Evan got married, nothing happened. Everything was fine, until their son, with whom Abby was pregnant before they married, was born, and three years later, fashioned his purple aura for the first time.

"Purple auras belonged to Brooks women, and there had never been a Reed man with the ability to manipulate all of the elements before. Only Brooks women could do that. That was the last day the Enchanters had their powers. That night, they were stripped of their elements and their auras and were nothing more than human."

"So the legend of the curse was wrong," Boyd speculated. "It was a child between the two who would kill the power?"

"No. It was just interpreted improperly. In those days, what was the only reason people got married?"

"To have sex. To have children."

"Exactly."

Boyd looked at Jett. "But the universe demands balance."

Jett nodded knowingly. "It took a lot of power to strip centuries of magic. As more of the powerless Enchanters bred with humans, since no one could tell the difference anymore, the universe got farther and farther away from balance. On the fullest moon of Chris's fifteenth year, the Enchanters had to get their power back in order to achieve the balance of what had been taking place for centuries.

"Of course that was against the curse, so instead, the magic stripped the Enchanters of the humanity that they'd been given back. It had no choice but to go backwards from the positive, reinforcing power they once had. Instead of the capacity to save another, the only power they would have would be to destroy."

"Enders," Boyd muttered.

"Enders," Jett agreed.

"So we kill all the Enchanters, and it all stops," Boyd guessed. "There will be nothing left of the bloodlines to manipulate."

Chris looked away from them, out the muddy train glass.

"Yes," Jett confirmed, squeezing Chris's hand. "We kill all the Enchanters, starting with Chris."

Boyd's face fell, a light traveling across his eyes. Boyd was a very intelligent human being despite his pothead nature, and Jett didn't have to wait long. He sat up straight, practically knocking Carmen off the seat.

"You still have the power," he said in a shock of enlightenment.

Chris didn't look at them.

"So the curse was wrong."

"No," Jett said quietly, as if Chris wouldn't hear her. "The curse had every intention of stripping everyone, including the prodigy child. But he was just too powerful for the Elders. With every inch of power at their disposal, they couldn't take him down."

"Which means he can take down the Enders."

"Maybe. But will the entire world fall with them? We don't know."

But Boyd didn't say what they were all thinking.

That the world had already fallen.

CHAPTER 9

THEY FELT LIKE A FUCKING ARMY.

They *were* a fucking army.

Combat boots pounding on the highway, the barrels of their guns cracked against their leather belts as they walked in unison. Beside him, Shea stopped when he heard nothing. The crew halted with them. To Devlin's knowledge, less than ten percent of the world's population—which had basically been wiped out—were Enders now because they really didn't have anything to eat, but Devlin's father was convinced that there was something to find off this stretch of highway.

Though he pretended well for the crew—no one but those who'd been there knew of Devlin's betrayal; they would all come after him and surely Shea wanted to be the one to take his son's life—he really had no idea where they were or where they were going. Shea apparently did, though.

Devlin had never known of any second cousin of his father's named Daniel who'd apparently been of a family named Wildes, son to a woman who'd been abandoned by her own family. Which, if you went back far enough, was more closely connected to the Shea family than anyone else. His grandmother, before she took the Shea family name, was Marni Clarke. Daniel, as Devlin pried out of his father, though named Linden, was known as a Clarke his entire life because of his appearance. Devlin didn't know anything about a person being given a different name based on what they looked like, but he couldn't get anything else out of his father.

Devlin didn't dare speak. He didn't dare do anything except glance at his father. Shea looked terrified. Which instantly terrified Devlin, because Shea wasn't scared of anything. Not usually. Devlin didn't reach for his gun, though. That'd likely just spook the rest of the crew.

No one spoke. Even if there were Enders, they didn't exactly want to call them over for dinner.

Devlin didn't have to wonder about setting up camp as the sun began to wander beneath the hill peak. Without warning, Shea pressed on, and Devlin presumed they'd be walking all night.

Which wasn't that disappointing.

* * *

"You guys go ahead," Jett said to Boyd and Carmen. "We'll catch up."

Carmen gave her sister a knowing look before hugging her. "I'll be right there," Jett promised in a whisper, which very well could have been a lie.

Boyd and Carmen disappeared slowly along the train tracks around a cluster of trees, and Jett placed her hands on Chris's bearded cheeks. She slid them slowly up his face and into his hair, pulling at the makeshift bun at the top of his head.

The vast possibility of the evening ocean expanded his chest with its calm waves; he tasted salt. He touched her soft cheek with the back of his fingertips, warming at the touch of his skin against hers. There was blue in her eyes.

"Where else are we going to go, Jetilyn?"

"I don't know. Does it matter? They'll die off eventually, or we will, but that is our choice to make."

Their heads snapped up as a deep voice filled the forest.

"Dev, take Carr with you."

At the sound of Shea's voice, Chris fiercely took hold of Jett's hand and led her backwards, the way they came. Unsheathing his knife from his belt, they leaned breathlessly against the trunk of a tree.

"To piss? Really?"

"It's not safe."

They heard nothing else as the sound of footsteps silenced. The Gunners were on the dirt, coming straight for them. Chris closed his eyes and produced a white light in his head.

"I'll wait here," the voice he presumed to belong to Carr said from a distance, and he heard Devlin's laugh.

Devlin appeared, unbuckling his belt, and Jett made a faint noise against the tree with her shoe. Devlin whirled, his buckle hanging off his jeans, a .45 pointed at Chris and Jett. She smiled an awkward smile as she tried not to look at Devlin's pants. Catching sight of them, he lowered his handgun and walked along the tracks. Jett and Chris followed silently.

Their whispers were so forced that Chris could barely hear them speak.

"How do they know where we're going?" Jett asked.

"I don't know," Devlin replied, rambling. "Something about Holies being responsible for the rise of the Enders, somebody named Daniel—"

In barely a moment's time, Chris found his hand around Devlin's neck whose blue eyes widened in fury. He didn't fight back. Yet. Jett didn't move.

"How do you know Daniel?" Chris demanded.

Devlin stared at him.

Chris couldn't breathe as he gazed upon Devlin. He gasped for air as the fact dawned on him that Devlin's appearance was identical to Chris's late uncle's.

His blue eyes. Black hair. Uncontrollable anger when crossed.

Devlin was a fucking Clarke.

But if that were the case, he would've taken up a career in cannibalism like the rest of them. Since he left Jasmyn, Chris had never seen another Enchanter who hadn't morphed into an Ender. But Devlin wasn't an Ender. So he couldn't be a Clarke. Could he?

Chris let go of him, looking down at the ground for a self-deprecating moment before he looked back up at Devlin Shea. "I'm sorry. Can you please tell me what you know about your family?"

"I'm a military brat," Devlin said. "I know nothing of my family except that I've been to more countries than you know the names of, and that my mother died of cancer when I was nine."

Chris nodded gently. "What do you know of Daniel?"

"That he was related to my father."

"Related how, exactly?"

"To Irina. And her sister Marni. Surname Clarke before she married Robert Shea, the second. Marni was my father's mother."

Chris hung his head as the realization hit him like a blow to the skull.

"Chris," Jett placed her hand on his shoulder. "Chris, who is Devlin—" she looked back and forth between the two guys, "who is he to you?"

Chris whooshed out a breath. "You have to come with us."

"What...I can't. Why?"

"Because you are *my* cousin. I'm responsible for you."

"What does that even mean?" Devlin stepped back in disbelief. "How are you responsible for me all of the sudden?"

"It means that you're a Healer. It means that you have the energy that you're an Enchanter, and it means that if you don't come with us right now, you will fucking die."

"I can't," Devlin refused. "If I do, *you* will fucking die."

With stomps of boots nearby—no doubt belonging to Robert Shea—Devlin left them standing there with nothing to say.

*　*　*

There was one type of Enchanter not told of in Jett's story to Boyd, not because of some secret but because it had been irrelevant at the time. The elemental power was only passed on to the strongest of the family who could physically and emotionally handle it, but that didn't mean those without the power were human.

Like Jett had told Boyd, Enchanter energy was in the blood. Members of the bloodline who weren't given the power still never got sick, and could still communicate with the energy like the Holies did, just on an extreme level in comparison to the Holies. Due to the strong, intuitive nature of these family members, they often became doctors or therapists, which earned them the label Healers. Because Devlin and his father were related to Chris's family, they were Healers.

Members of the Enchanter family were born Healers, but they couldn't become powerful Enchanters until they sparked, which meant that their aura became visible to other Enchanters for the first time and they could begin using their power. Some Healers never sparked for the course of their lifetime, which is why they were called Healers instead of Enchanters. If they were going to spark, it was typically in the first ten years of life. They were called Healers until they sparked, or until they died from old age.

Chris had been three when he sparked, which was what signaled the inception of the centuries-old curse. There had been only one person who ever sparked later in life, in his thirties. His name was Elias Linden of the Hadley family — who controlled fire — and he was Chris's grandfather. No one ever found out why he sparked late.

Devlin could spark, then. Especially now, being surrounded by an Enchanter of his close family. Sparking, Jett knew from Chris, was a very painful experience, the pain escalating with every year the Enchanter grows. It hadn't been nearly as bad for Chris being of young age as it had been for Elias.

Once upon a time, Chris had explained it to Jett like if someone were to cut you open from head to toe, set your organs and your bones and your heart and your intestines on fire, and then stitch you back up for you to burn from the inside out. The guilt of this possibly happening to Devlin with Chris not there to help him was eating at him already.

Chris's family, the Reeds, were protectors. They had been since the beginning of time. Jett knew that she should flip the switch and block out Chris's energy that was black and cloudier every second, but she couldn't rationalize leaving him alone to his own darkness.

Hand in hand and breathless, they caught up to Carmen and Boyd at the edge of the tracks, which meant they were in Hazel.

"Thank the stars," Chris breathed, and everyone looked at him like he'd just said he ate children for sport.

"Enchanter expression." He cleared his throat. "We don't believe in God."

Holies didn't believe in God either, but they didn't have special expressions since they weren't supposed to talk.

Hazel Grove wasn't the beauty it had once been. When Jett's parents were her age, Hazel was known for its Victorian beauty. At any time of the day or night, downtown would be bustling with people of all ages, down the sidewalk that was lined with lit trees and horse carriages on either side.

There were no horses, dead or alive, to be found now. The lights on the trees had long gone out, and there wasn't a being—human or otherwise—to be seen. They could barely see the long dilapidated buildings that closed them in on the street without the stars. That didn't stop Chris from staring up at the art gallery on the left side of the street, though.

The Valentine, an iconic monument for Chris's family, was where his grandfather Elias had his first date with his grandmother Jane. From Chris's lips, it was told like a modern Cinderella story. And there was no Cinderella as beautiful as Jane Wildes. At least, in her Enchanter form. Her Ender form that they had encountered back in the woods in Reynan was a painful sight to say the least. Jett couldn't imagine what that must have been like for Chris.

Their moment turned purple as urgency boomed in Jett's chest, as much as she would have liked to give Chris the moment he so clearly needed.

"What's going on?" Carmen asked.

"Gunners are coming to Jasmyn. Right now."

CHAPTER 10

FROM LILIAN HIGHWAY into the woods, through a narrow pathway lined with pink flowers, the three Holies and one Enchanter arrived, what seemed to be, in time. At the edge of the pathway, the three Holies halted. As the sound of footsteps waned behind him, Chris turned around.

"Shit."

In its day, Jasmyn Lake was *alive*. Like all elements when they came in contact with Enchanters, the lake itself had the power to change forms, to manipulate other elements around it. If an outsider—someone who wasn't an Enchanter—entered the forest town of Jasmyn Lake, they would begin to feel fear. The trees would appear larger than they were, and the breeze would chill them to the bone. No human ever stayed longer than a couple minutes out of fear that the woods would swallow them whole. It was Jasmyn's way of keeping out those who didn't belong.

But that wasn't the case now.

The pink flowers that lined the pathway were azaleas which translated into *home*, or *thinking of home bush*. It was true that, in the presence of an azalea bush, Enchanters could see their future. Whether they would be married, or have children, or live happily. But Chris wasn't expecting Holies to see anything. They were human, after all.

Based on the glaze of their eyes as they stood frozen on the pathway, they were seeing something Chris was not. He waited. He'd already seen his future many years ago when walking this path, which was why he'd brought that girl from Hazel Grove home to his parents that one evening when he was sixteen for pancakes. Little did he know that there was a girl in Devonbrook who looked astonishingly similar to her, and her name was not Michelle Hanby. Her name was Jetilyn Fournier.

It was unfortunate, in Chris's case, that the azaleas had shown him the wrong future. If it hadn't, he wouldn't have kissed Jett in The Nowhere Train the first night he brought her there just after he told her the entire Enchanter story, and she probably wouldn't have revolted against him and told him never to touch her again, and he probably wouldn't be painfully in love with her, and he probably wouldn't care that she was emotionally chasing after a Gunner who just happened to be his cousin.

That is what he was telling himself, anyway. That it was all the fucking azaleas' fault.

Their epiphanic precognition behind them, while Boyd and Carmen looked at each other, Jetilyn looked at Chris.

As powerful as his inner turmoil was, a sensual warmth filled his chest as he watched the world turn bright pink, and his stomach dropped with the force of a sack of bricks. It nearly took him off his feet.

"What did you see?" he whispered.

Jett indulged in another long moment to stare dumbfounded at him, and then she walked right past him into a large clearing before a blue cabin with a silver door.

*   *   *

"You cannot just stand out in the open like this," Chris whispered urgently, abandoning Holie rule with his voice. They were in his town now, and he didn't have time for their hippie bullshit right now.

"For generations every Ench—" Chris let his mouth droop open as his words trailed off.

Grayson gawked at him sternly. He didn't know the whole story, but he knew enough. The rest of them didn't know shit, though.

"It's not safe," Chris recovered. "There are likely to be more Enders in a remote location like this."

It was as if they also lost their hearing when they gave up their voices. No one moved an inch or even seemed to understand what he'd just said.

Chris sighed, looking to Grayson. Grayson said nothing.

"There's a cabin at the top of the hill. It's an ideal vantage point. It's large, so most of you can fit. Two or three will fit fine in the small yellow cabin right behind Jasmyn, just a short walk east. Raina," Chris said to the only woman with small children, "there's a green cabin just a couple hundred feet that way. It has three bedrooms. There's a large tree—the only one with orange leaves—take a left there. You can't miss it. Boyd, Carmen, Jett, Dama, you're with me."

Chris grabbed Jett's wrist and practically dragged her through the small crowd and past the cracking picket fence. He felt the electricity of the energy pass back and forth behind his back, but he ignored it. He tore open the silver door of the cabin, and, as he knew he would at any second, he broke at the sight of the violet room. His knees cracked the floor as he knelt in front of his childhood. His grandparents had died young, but he had spent more time here with his parents and his aunt and uncle than he had in the green cottage, which was his parents' place.

His grandmother Jane had been an eccentric soul, like her grandmother before her. She'd been superstitious about the sunlight since everything bad that ever happened to her happened during the day, so she had the darkest purple material possible made into curtains. Her purple candles, her incense, her glass vases filled with flowers long dead, were baked with a thick dust. Over the brick fireplace was a painting of *Starry Night* by Van Gogh. It'd portrayed just what Jasmyn looked like at night. Jane's grandmother, Annabelle, had given it to her just before she died. It was Elias's favorite painting.

Chris's eyes began to strain as he glared at the painting in front of him, but he couldn't summon the strength to blink them closed. His memory of his parents' skin drooping and flaking off onto their clothes clutched around his heart and it wouldn't let go.

It had taken him so long to kill them then, in comparison to how quickly he could take down an Ender now. He had lived such a human life, with dinner at the table and a girlfriend and real school and parties, while hiding the secret from his parents that he could actually still fashion; he could actually kill without ever using his hands. With his hesitation in that moment in his living room those years ago, they could have easily eaten him. But miraculously, he'd gotten out.

He'd gotten out, and he'd sworn to himself that he'd never come back.

As the sting of his tears on his cheeks awoke him from the memory, he felt Boyd's hands on him. He didn't have the emotional strength to tell Boyd to take them to another room, any other room, so this one it was.

He fell asleep in the dirty purple sheets, the oil painting on the wall the last thing he saw.

Devlin really did look like Daniel. They could be twins.

* * *

Jett's skin boiled red hot as Dama walked into the kitchen. Enders. Jett lifted her forehead from the kitchen table where she'd collapsed.

"Your dad wants to know what to do with them," Dama said quietly.

Glaring at the center of Dama's forehead, Jett gave her back the red.

"Kill them all," Dama said agreeably. "Got it."

* * *

Chris awoke to Jett kissing him. He opened himself up to her, digging his fingertips into her hips and crushing her to him. Her tongue was comfortably warm, but her guilt was setting her existence on fire.

He grabbed her lightly by the shoulder and pulled away.

Her eyes filled with tears. She wept, blinking them away. "I'm sorry. I'm just a human girl, and I know that's the shittiest excuse ever, but I never knew this life like you did. I was scared."

"Scared of me?"

"Yes? No? I don't know."

He let her go. "Which is it, Jetilyn?"

She bundled up the collar of his shirt in her fist and brought him close again. "I didn't want to lose you. Not like that. Not in this fucked up world we're living in. I wanted to have you as long as I had myself, and if I admitted that I was in love with you and I lost you, I would lose myself, and then I would have neither of us."

Her fist released and she got up, to leave him, again, but he grabbed the back of her dress like he had done with her shirt, ripping it as he pulled her back. He rolled himself over her, snaking his hand up her thigh and squeezing, hard. He kissed her like he'd never kissed anyone and like he would never kiss again; he kissed her like she was dying and he was dying and this was going to be his last taste on this earth or on any earth.

She bit his lip, forcing him into a groan, and he cursed, remembering their company in the very next room, probably, and she told him that Carmen and Dama and Boyd had left, and no one was there, and her hands were on his belt and then they were stroking the stiffness in his jeans that was really not going away any time soon.

In a vibration against his lips, she giggled as he failed to smoothly get her dress over her head, and it was already ripped, so he ripped the cotton from the hem all the way up to her neck. To his knowledge, they hadn't been to the lingerie section in a fucking *Target* lately, and her breasts therefore gazed up at him in all their perky glory. She giggled some more as he struggled to get his jeans off his long legs, but the humor stopped as soon as he kissed her neck, his fingers sliding to the cotton underwear that was already soaked through.

"Jetilyn," he said, and his lips slid down her body, taking one of her breasts in his mouth, biting down gently on her nipple. She wailed out a moan, the second half of which caught in her throat as his fingers pushed the cotton of her underwear aside and thrust inside her. She was apparently having a hard time breathing.

He decided not to rip those as well—who knew how many she had, probably just this one pair—but slid them down as far as he could get them without his tongue leaving the wetness between her legs. Her hands tugged at his long hair as her body began to shake, and he stopped.

"*No,*" she begged desperately.

"Yes," he countered, and he slide higher and thrust himself into her.

She gasped, her body arching and rising off the bed. The back of her head followed suit, digging into the pillows so he couldn't see her eyes, as he slid himself deeply inside her in a rhythm that was nothing if not hasty. Her hands gripped his lower back, and her hips danced with him as she pulled him as deeply into her as was possible, and then deeper. Her legs intertwined over his shoulders and behind his neck, and when he teased at her inner thigh with his bite, she screamed. He didn't exactly pride himself on his minute-mandom, but as her orgasm dripped down his thighs, he came, tugging on her hair and growling like he was a beast and she his dinner.

Collapsing on top of her, his words were muted by her hair that smelled like dirt and ocean air.

"Hmmm?" she moaned sleepily.

"I need to swim," he said into her ear. "Right now. You don't have to come."

"What if I want to come?" she whispered, and they laughed.

He kissed her forehead. "I will show you the real Jasmyn."

"Is she still alive?"

"I don't know."

CHAPTER 11

CHRIS DIDN'T GET TO SWIM right away, but he would be proven wrong about the state of this place.

There were no Enders there. Not a single one.

In a few hours, Grayson and the family had run the perimeter, cleared the cabins, and checked the lake, and there was not one living-dead creature to be found. There was nothing to be found. No one was there.

Grayson met Chris outside of Jane and Elias's old cabin to tell him all of this, obviously privy to the fact that Chris had just fucked the shit out of his daughter. Even if she could hide from her father the serene energy coursing through her, she couldn't hide the fact that she wore one of Jane's old sundresses, which were not even close to her flowy, hippie style. Or her sex hair.

Grayson smiled at her, and she crossed her arms, failing at hiding her smile all the way, so that a half smirk embellished her beautiful face.

"What are you smiling about?" she asked her father.

"You two must've been *very* distracted. You haven't noticed?"

"What?"

In response, Grayson looked up to the dark sky, his head hanging there for an indeterminate amount of time.

Mirroring him, Jett and Chris looked up.

The night sky was an explosion of white light. It sparkled down on them like Disneyland on Christmas.

There were fucking stars here.

Chris laughed. He laughed until his stomach hurt, and he grabbed Jett's hand and they were running through the woods.

The wind burned her hot cheeks.

"Slow down!" she begged, laughing. "I'm going to run into a tree."

"No, you're not," he said, weaving through the woods like it was an open road. "I know these woods like nothing you've ever known."

"Where are we going?" she asked, and nearly toppled over from the momentum as they halted suddenly.

She could stay silent for fifty years and still not have a ready word to say. Every breath she could ever take was yanked out of her by the real Jasmyn, as Chris so admirably called it.

Their feet hung halfway over the edge of a cliff that overlooked a lake so dark it appeared more violet than it did blue. The crisp surface mirrored the sparkle of the stars in Jett's eyes. She blinked at them and they smiled.

Jett took a step off the cliff, and any fall was broken by gigantic white boulders lined like an army to protect what lay within.

Chris let go of her hand as she stepped forward. She looked back at him with this smile that sort of hurt her face.

She watched his honey eyes glaze with contentment as she posed him the question with blue oceans and skies of teal. He slowly shook his head 'no' as skies turned to purple in her head. What she saw was what was in front of her and what would be in front of her someday, if the azaleas were correct. If they survived, that is.

Jasmyn was not safe. Jasmyn was not safe, exactly, but she wasn't dangerous either. Not to Jett. But Jett had thrown safe out the window about an hour ago, and Chris knew that.

She jumped in.

*   *   *

The Gunners trekked the long way around the woods of Jasmyn Lake to the east side because Shea thought that the Holies would be expecting them if they came in through the highway. Though Devlin really didn't give a shit about any of the men and women he and his father ran with, he worried for them more with every step they took. They seemed to be in some type of trance as they looked up at the tall trees that lined the forest. Even their normally-synced marching behind him was haphazard and out of order. It was as if their boots were disintegrating right off their feet.

He couldn't understand their reaction to this place even as he looked up and saw what they saw. The sky above the tips of the tall evergreens was bursting with the kind of light that none of them had seen in years. Having barely remembered what they looked like but wishing for this sight at least once more in the short lifetime he probably had left, it felt like a wet dream that he hadn't quite woken up from.

But he didn't fear it like the rest of them—his father included—seemed to. He wanted to touch them. He wanted to stop and let this be the last thing he ever saw.

Stars.

The night was so fucking beautiful.

"I can't," were the words that Devlin heard behind him while at the same time in front of him, his father stepped onto the dirt from the highway.

Shea sunk his hands into his pockets to stop them from shaking. There was only one thing that the words *I can't* translated to in the language of Shea and that was *Iamgoingtobeatthefuckoutofyou.*

Shea turned on the heel of his boot without a moment's notice and had his grungy hand in the woman's hair in 0.6 seconds.

"Don't ever tell me you can't," Shea growled, and pushed her into the woods.

No one else, Devlin included, *especially* Devlin, dared to say a word.

*   *   *

The lake was *purple*. Jett would have described it as this blackened purple when she first saw it but now, it was a real purple.

Glitter shimmered like a blanket over the surface, catching the sparkle of the stars in the dark sky above.

"What is that?" Jett said incredulously, holding Chris's hand in the water.

If her eyes were photographic and could capture the swirl the color made as she ran her fingertips through the water, she would've snapped a thousand pictures.

Chris's warmth enveloped her chest, even in the cool water.

"No," she said with her own disbelief caught in her throat. "Auras don't *look* like that, Chris. They're solid and blurry and...no. It can't be."

"That's what a real aura looks like," he said softly, raising her hand to his lips. "In my world. You just can't see it on me because I'm human. This is the only way I can show it to you. To stretch it onto another Enchanted being. In this case, Jasmyn."

"And yours is purple?"

"Yes," he nodded. "The only male Enchanter in history with a purple aura."

Suddenly, Chris looked up to the sky, and the color in the water disappeared in a whirlwind towards them, as if it had been vacuumed out. The light of the stars began to fade as the sky went black.

"What's happening?" Jett asked him, squeezing his hand.

"You can't feel that?"

Jett felt nothing.

"Too far yet," Chris said calmly, "but they're here."

"Gunners? How many?"

"All of them."

CHAPTER 12

"DON'T BOTHER," CHRIS'S VOICE boomed from the trees, and he stepped out onto the clearing in front of the blue cottage.

Holies stood clustered at the far edge, gathering the small number of weapons they had, which were basically just rusted pocket knives.

None of them would answer him, especially Grayson, but they would listen. That's all Holies did, really. Listen. Which is why they were so smart.

Grayson's daughter stood with Chris, against him and their family, as she spoke words that he'd never before allowed her to speak.

"Carmen," Jett said, looking at her sister, clad in what was once their mother's clothes. "Get in the house. You too, Boyd. And you, Dama."

"No," Carmen refused.

"Yes," Jett ordered sternly.

Looking down, Carmen disappeared into the front silver door without another word, followed by Boyd and Dama.

"I'll take them down quickly," Chris promised. "If that makes you uncomfortable, you're welcome to go your own way. But if you do not want to stay, I need to know now. The boy belongs to me, and I need all of you who stay to be on my side so that I can save him."

Grayson cleared his throat, and the group stared at him in shock as if he'd just said he'd been raised by werewolves.

"What does that mean, Christopher? How does he belong to you?"

Grayson could read the truth out of Devlin if he really wanted to, but he didn't really want to.

"Devlin Shea is my cousin, Grayson. His grandmother and mine grew up together in the same house in Reynan."

"And his father, the Gunner, he is also related to you?"

"Technically, yes. But he's not one of my family. He's a snake, and had my grandmother Jane known about him when she was alive, she would have killed him."

"And you will kill him now?"

"Providing you don't stand in my way, yes."

"And if we do?"

"Then I will kill you first. All of you. I have to protect my people. What's left of them."

Jett looked up at him but Chris did not look at her. Grayson half-expected her to walk away from him or slap him, but she did nothing of the sort. Holies knew no loyalty like Enchanters. The word didn't even have the same meaning to humans.

"Then we will stand with you."

"No you won't. You will all disappear into the homes I have given you until it is safe to come out."

"And my daughter?"

"Have you ever tried to tell Jetilyn Fournier what to do, Grayson?"

At that, Grayson laughed. He spared one glance at his people, and they all disappeared into the trees.

"I will stay," he told his adopted son. "Kill me if you like."
Bluff called.

Chris took a deep breath, and held Jetilyn tight against his side. "I could never kill you, Grayson. You are my family, too."

* * *

They rolled in like fucking SWAT.

Fully loaded AR-15s drawn and firing the heat of death, they masked their fear behind the soul of Samuel Colt himself.

For about 0.26 seconds. Until the bullets came to a halt in mid-air and fell to the ground.

"What the fuck." Devlin heard his own voice and felt his lips move but had no intention of saying anything.

He looked at his father. Shea did not look surprised. His arm dropped, dragging the barrel of his rifle in the dirt. His fingers clenched around it. He was pissed, but he was not surprised.

Devlin looked back up to the clearing where they stood with at least fifteen of their best shooters. The bullets hadn't exactly just fallen to the ground. They had... bounced. Off.

Through a blurry mist of white, Devlin squinted to see Jett, Chris, and Jett's father, whom Devlin had saved from the Ender in Malibu.

The white...wall...thing... looked to be a collection of stars in mid-air that could deter fucking a .223.

As quickly as it had appeared in front of the Holie trio, the misty wall fell into a million shards of glitter and disappeared into the dirt.

Shea raised his gun, pointing it at Chris's forehead, who stood ahead of both Jett and Grayson, and Chris smiled.

The guy was a fucking sociopath.

Devlin racked his brain for what to do to save Jett as he was sure she would do for him, but he didn't have the chance. This place was seriously fucked up.

Out of the corner of his eye, Devlin saw his father, the unstoppable, indestructible controller of his entire life, go flying into the air, tossed *over the trees* and who knows where the hell else.

Chris had turned purple. His entire body was surrounded in the same kind of mist that had formed the wall separating them, except in this shiny violet color that sprayed against the night air like a cloud. Devlin dropped his gun in the dirt and glared at this alien person. Chris's arms were bare in the tank top he wore, and Devlin watched thick steam come off his skin, like some kind of mutant from a comic book.

His trance broke when Jett ran in front of Chris, straight for Devlin. She grabbed his hand and pulled him into the front yard of a blue cottage to his right.

"Jett, what in the—"

A crash in the clearing stole his words, and he watched in awe from the front porch. Jett's father joined them, but Devlin hardly noticed.

In a sudden downpour the likes of which Devlin had never seen in California, trees began to fall. The earth itself cracked. In the aftermath of an earthquake that was over almost as quickly as it began, there was a linear crater between the house and the trees across the clearing that could swallow every person here whole. In the middle of it all, straddling the crack between his legs, stood Chris in all his violet glory, like...like a fucking god.

Across from him, the Gunners looked like they had when they arrived: scared shitless. Those who reacted quickly enough to run, at least three of them, got picked off by lightning bolts striking from the sky.

Regardless of the death and murder and regardless of every inhumane atrocity Devlin had ever witnessed in the shadow of his father, his stomach began to roll, pushing bile up to his throat. His arms began to shake as pain set in. His bones were expanding inside his body, threatening to break through his skin. He looked down at his hands which were stark white, and he watched Chris's steam rise from his own pores. He gasped for air, but it wasn't enough. He couldn't breathe.

"Dev?" Jett asked him, placing her warm hand on his shoulder. "Dev, are you okay?"

His mouth gaped open, but nothing came out except a choking noise. His insides were strangling him.

"Chris!" Jett screamed louder than anything he could ever imagine coming out of her, and their eyes met.

The white spots before Devlin's eyes cleared, and the pain subsided enough that he could sort of breathe.

Wind.

Devlin lifted his face to the heavy blast that seemed to be swirling around his head. He breathed deeply, as if oxygen could only be found in that windstorm.

He lowered his eyes to Chris, twenty feet away. The wind whooshed against Devlin's face. He stared directly at Chris. The harder the wind came, the more the brighter purple form flickered.

Devlin didn't understand the world in that moment, but he wanted death to be much less painful. He'd always thought it would be.

"Hold on," Chris growled over the wind and the rain. "I just need you to stay alive for five minutes."

With that, Chris turned back to the Gunners Devlin had brought with him, and the earth resumed its shattering under their feet. Chris took advantage of their confusion and their fear, and he approached them, knife in hand, and began to pick them off. Like it had with the white mist, their gunfire bounced off his violet shield.

He went for the head like Devlin might with Enders, sinking his knife into the brains of Shea's people one by one.

Some ran, but Chris didn't bother with them. They would never dream of coming back.

The rain stopped suddenly, and Devlin shuddered at the sight of Chris standing among a pile of dead bodies at his feet, blood dripping from the tip of the knife in his hand, an image that would be forever frozen in his memory.

Devlin's throat closed up again, albeit by a different force.

His father, limping bloody and broken with one of his arms hanging dead from its socket, emerged from the woods.

Chris dropped his knife and glared at the old military vet.

Without warning, Robert Shea burst into flames. Chris did not end his misery quickly. He let the King of the Gunners wail through the flames as he burned alive and then died, a pile of broken bones and ash.

EPILOGUE

"DEVLIN," CHRIS APPROACHED him carefully, looking like a human again, like Devlin was some sort of animal that should be caged. That was about how he felt right then. "Devlin, I'm sorry I had to do that."

Not making a sound, Jett stepped aside.

Devlin shook his head, shivering "It's—" he stuttered "—he would've killed me anyway."

"Do you trust me?" Chris asked.

"Not really."

"Can you trust me for the next fifteen minutes?"

"Do I have a choice?"

"Not really."

Devlin felt himself sort of smile.

"We are going to climb on the roof."

"I'm sorry, what?"

"I promise I'll explain everything to you in a moment, but right now, I need to get you up as high as I can in the shortest amount of time I can. Or else you're going to die."

"What's happening to me?"

"You're sparking."

Devlin blinked and tears of pain bled down his cheeks. "What does that mean?"

"It means we're family. Come with me, please. I'll take care of you. I promise."

THE END

Turn the page for an exclusive excerpt of Prius, Vol. 2 of The Enders, coming late summer 2015 from Booktrope Editions.

PRIUS

THERE WEREN'T ANY BLACKBOARDS in Christian Reed's house, last time he checked.

There weren't any bears, either. They did live in the woods, but they never seemed to run into any animals. Maybe Cameron had eaten them all before he died.

The low growls accompanying the screech of evil that filled his house were not sounds that were familiar to Chris. He could tell you how the breeze sounded different under a tree than out in the clearing in front of his late grandparents' house, how many times his girlfriend Michelle breathed on his face before she fell asleep each night.

He had no idea what this sound was, only that it was getting louder and closer with each gaining second.

He opened his eyes to find Michelle sleeping beside him on the same bed his mother Abby and father Evan had conceived him. He tried not to think about that too much, but he usually failed. To this day, he was still very in love with the Romeo and Juliet story that was his parents' marriage. Michelle's blue eyes flickered under her eyelids with every step that the sound took closer to them, and he found himself wondering, if only just for a moment, why she had blue eyes. The azaleas had lied to him about her, he realized, when it was much too late. They had never done that before, and he had yet to figure out why. Flowers didn't lie. Usually.

Swiftly but quietly, Chris halfway rolled his body over his girlfriend's, shaking her with an urgent whisper in her ear. "We have to—"

Chris instinctively crossed his arms over Michelle's face, protecting her, as a crash exploded his tiny universe. His sandy brown eyes rose slowly to find his mother, who was not his mother at all, but a, um…monster. Usually they reserved that word for Clarkes, but his uncle Daniel would appreciate it, Chris thought, if he had been here.

Chris's mother Abby, once known in Chris's mind as the most beautiful woman to walk the earth, looked like she had rubbed her face against the trunk of a tree until it fell off. The skin that was left hanging off her cheekbones were plastered with some combination of blood, dirt, and… pancake mix, maybe. The unruly growling screech from a moment before was now echoing from the back of Abby's throat, as her mouth drooped open like some kind of cartoon character. (He guessed from his father's childhood stories. They didn't have a television. Never had.)

In a science fiction horror movie—Chris guessed again: he'd only seen two films in his life—he would expect for the 'zombie'—in this case his mother—would immediately go for his pretty face. (He wasn't a narcissist but it was a well-known fact that all Enchanters were stunningly beautiful, especially the men.) But she didn't. Her tar black—once the most luminous emerald green—eyes twitched inside her skull as she tilted her head at him. As if her brain had forgotten how to tell her legs to walk, she wobbled on her feet, seemingly failing at deciding whether or not to eat him.

He held her unfamiliar gaze as he pushed on Michelle's hip, urging her to escape out the window behind him. Amidst the rustle of the sheets as she slid herself down the bed beside him, he inched himself closer to Abby. Michelle's bare feet hit the carpet, and Chris no longer had to wonder if his mother had any motor skills left.

Like a ninja who had traded her stealth for the indigenous trudge of Godzilla, zombiefied Abby stomped calculatedly towards Chris's sixteen-year-old girlfriend. Even if Chris thought he could, he wasn't sure if he would save that human life in that moment. He, along with every male member of his family, had for generations been bred to protect their mothers at all costs. Even if she had, with the threat of imminent death, attacked him, he wouldn't ever lay a hand on his mother. Never, ever. He wouldn't. He couldn't. Ever.

Michelle didn't even fight back. As she caught wind of the reality that the zombie was at her back instead of across the room, she whirled, and she screamed. The blood-curdling cry only made it halfway out of her tiny body before she froze when Abby's teeth took a chunk out of her neck. Michelle went down, convulsing, and Abby indulged in the apparent opportunity to eat her from the outside in. Chris watched his mother eat his girlfriend. He supposed he could have got up in that moment and walked out, but he didn't. He didn't really love Michelle all that much—'I love you too' was just what teenage guys were supposed to say when their girlfriends professed their irrevocable love—but he didn't think she deserved to die, especially like that. Regardless, he didn't save her, and he didn't really care that she was dying. As much as he had spent his entire life hiding his inhumanity from the world, he admitted to himself that right now that all he really cared about was his mother, why she had transformed into a monster, and what he could do to save her.

Having had her fill, Chris guessed, Abby rose from her knees, blood dripping from her chin. Chris paid the half-chewed intestines sprawling from Michelle's body no mind as he watched his mother walk out of his bedroom without another glance his way.

He had to leave. He had nowhere to go, but obviously, he had to leave before he turned into one of them or before he was eaten by one of them and then turned into one of them.

Like his father would once upon a time, and his father's father before him, he leaped out the window in the swiftest, unconscious motion. He weaved his way through the woods that he knew as sure as he knew his own name, halting at the edge of the trees.

As he always did, as they all always did, Chris reveled at the sparkling stars in the black sky for a short selfish moment before he crossed the line from the trees to Lilian Highway. He had a strange intuition that it was the last time he was going to see any sky like this for a while.

For the first time in his life, Christian Reed ran, and he never looked back.

ALSO BY ALLIE BURKE

Paper Souls (Literary Fiction) A dark, heartbreaking tour told through the surreal psychosis of Schizophrenia, of how the irreparably damaged and broken survive.

Violet Midnight (Paranormal Romance) A powerful enchantress meets a handsome man with a painful past, and so begins a love story that will change the world as they know it, forever.

Emerald Destiny (Paranormal Romance) Young, handsome Evan has loved forbidden Abby since childhood, but is his passion strong enough to overcome the forces working to keep them apart.

Amber Passion (Paranormal Romance) Can the enchanting Claire soothe Daniel's darkness as he yearns for her without even realizing it as he mourns a separation from his twin sister?

The Enchanters Collection (Paranormal Romance Collection) This genre-defining trilogy weaves the beautiful complexity of true love through auras, darkness, and magic.

MORE GREAT READS
FROM BOOKTROPE

The Appeal of Evil by **Pembroke Sinclair** (Paranormal Romance) Katie wants to invest her heart and soul in love, but she may lose both to Hell when she falls for devilishly charming Josh—who happens to be a demon from Hell. Torn between two loves, Katie must choose sides in an epic battle of good versus evil.

The Lycan Hunter by **Kelsey Jordan** (Paranormal Romance) Alexis, a top-rated Hunter, meets Kyran, the handsome Alpha Lycan. Their chance encounter and a desperate prophecy forever change the future of the pack and the outcome of the 8000-year war.

The Soul Thief by **Majanka Verstraete** (Paranormal Fiction) 16-year-old Riley must come to terms with being a Halfling Angel of Death while battling an evil force that has murdered several girls her age, knowing she'll be next…

Blood & Spirits by **Dennis Sharpe** (Paranormal) Small-town life can be hard for a dead girl. A raucous ride through the dangerous lives of the lecherous undead.

CPSIA information can be obtained at www.ICGtesting.com
Printed in the USA
BVOW04s0610160315

391695BV00001B/1/P